TALES OF THE
MODERN WEST

ALSO BY FRED G. BAKER

FICTION
The Black Freighter
Life, Death, and Espionage by Paul *******:
Lena's Secret War
The Final Wave

ZONA: The Forbidden Land
Einstein's Raven

The Detective Sanchez/Father Montero Mysteries:
An Imperfect Crime
Desert Sanctuary
Desert Underworld

The Modern Pirate Series:
Seizing the Tiger	*Prowling Tiger*
Restless Tiger	*Raging Tiger*
Hong Kong Takedown	*The Good Deed/Chen*

Caribbean Queen/The Exchange/Venezuela Nights
Grenada Blood and Nazi Treasure

NON-FICTION
Growing Up Wisconsin:
The Life and Times of Con James Baker
of Des Moines, Chicago and Wisconsin

The Ancestors of Con James Baker of
Des Moines, Iowa, and Chicago, Illinois,
Volumes I–III

The Descendants of John Baker (ca. 1640–1704) of Hartford,
Connecticut, Through Thirteen Generations,
Volumes I-II

Light from a Thousand Campfires:
with Hannah Pavlik

Tales of the Modern West

Collected Short Stories

Fred G. Baker

Other Voices Press
Golden, Colorado

Published by Other Voices Press, Golden, Colorado
ISBN 978-1-949336-32-0 paperback
ISBN 978-1-949336-33-7 e-book

Cover design by Nick Zelinger, nz graphics
All rights reserved by Fred G. Baker.

Printed in the United States.

Acknowledgments

I would like to thank the following people for their aid and support in the writing and production of this book:

Dr. Hannah Pavlik, for her support and encouragement.

Donna Zimmerman, for her word processing and interior design contributions.

Nick Zelinger, for the cover design.

My beta readers, who provided helpful comments and ideas.

Contents

Introduction

T*ales of the Modern West* contains ten stories, some short and some long, of events that take place primarily in the Rocky Mountain states of America. They were written over a twelve-year period. In "Old Blue and the Avalanche," readers are introduced to retired Marine Corps Sergeant Hardy Harris and his faithful basset hound, Old Blue. Blue is a rescue dog who found Hardy when he needed a companion, and they have been inseparable ever since. The story describes what happens when the two are forced to transport a school bus full of kids across treacherous Red Mountain Pass in the rugged southwest Colorado mountains during a winter blizzard.

Hardy and Blue return in "Black Storm on White Mountain," a tale of modern horse rustling in the vast mountainous terrain of western Wyoming. Stormy, the wild black stallion, has to defend his herd of mares from a gang of modern-day horse thieves, and the dynamic duo help set things straight.

"Her Side of the Story" reveals the innate humanity in mountain villagers when an ancient Ute woman steps forward at a funeral to claim a keepsake belonging to the man she loves. In "Talkeetna Blues," a young man reflects on the aftereffects of excessive celebration on Midsummer Eve. An encounter with a grizzly bear describes what it can be like to live in the wilderness in "Night Breeze: The Bear" and "Night Breeze: Reprisal."

The lighter side of mountain living is depicted in "At the Forest Queen Hotel" and "A Night in Old Durango."

A daring robbery and hostage crisis in Rifle, Colorado, are recounted in "The Rifle Stickup." Cowboys rise to the occasion in the modern day and save the damsel in distress, much as they would have in earlier times.

Finally, "Chasing Cattle" is a tale about what it was like to be a ranch hand only a few years ago on the plains of Wyoming.

These stories provide a glimpse into the richness of life in western mountain towns and illustrate the character of those who live there. From good-natured people to outlaws, they all give you a flavor of the modern West.

Old Blue and the Avalanche

Retired US Marine Corps Sergeant Hardy Harris had about had his fill of his current orders. He had just been informed that they were going to drive up and over Red Mountain Pass and back to Durango through a snowstorm that evening.

"Mrs. Reynolds," he had pleaded, "you don't seem to understand. I've driven over that pass a dozen times in snow, and it can be dangerous."

"No, Mr. Harris," Reynolds said sternly, "you don't understand. We *are* going home, or you'll be looking for a new job tomorrow." Hardy didn't think it was safe, but she paid him no mind. She had gone off to find the children and assemble them at the parking lot for boarding on his yellow Blue Bird school bus, whether he liked it or not. Hardy had one last chance to talk some sense into Reynolds, but he had to find Lori Phillips first to get her support.

It had all started out well this morning when they had left Durango, Colorado, for the seventy-mile drive north to Ouray for the day. The outing had been planned for weeks and had a tight schedule. The fourteen Cub Scouts; Mrs. Lori Phillips, the den mother; and Mrs. Martha Reynolds, the wife of a school board member, had all been excited about the trip to spend a day at the famous water park in downtown Ouray. The Ouray Hot Springs Pool was developed by the town into a large swimming area, water slide, and hot pool for residents and visitors to enjoy. The scouts had a great time during the day, eating a picnic lunch in the middle of winter, lolling in the warm water, and playing water polo and other games. But a little after noon, snow clouds had moved in from the west, indicating that the storm front originally predicted for the middle of the night had arrived early.

The first flurries began to fall by three o'clock, and Hardy lobbied to start heading back as soon as possible to avoid any heavy snow on the road. He had navigated snowy roads for decades and had driven school buses for many of those years in weather fair and foul, especially in deep snow in South Dakota, where he was born and raised. He knew that the big yellow school buses were safe normally, but they did not handle well in snow, even with tire chains. And tonight there would be heavy snow—lots of it.

If the weather reports were anywhere near accurate, which was a mighty big *if*, the storm could drop up to a foot of the white powder in a few hours. He did not relish the idea of struggling along in the dark over the notorious Red Mountain Pass, known for its tight turns and steep inclines and, especially, avalanches. This time of year, there were always *small* avalanches, enough to block the road and cover it in several feet of packed snow before the slide continued over the side of the road and down the mountain. If you got caught in one, especially a *big* one, as it crossed the road, it could bury your car or truck, leaving you to freeze if help wasn't near or just sweep you off the road altogether, in the worst-case scenario.

Anyway, Hardy didn't like it. He went into the lobby of the Ouray Hot Springs Pool Visitors Center to look for Lori, a sensible woman whose son was one of the scouts. She would be reasonable, he was sure, and maybe the two of them could then convince Mrs. Reynolds that it would be safer to take the road over to Placerville and out to Cortez on the way to Durango. It was a much longer route, at about 170 miles versus seventy miles over the pass, or four to five hours instead of two hours at night, but it crossed no major roadways that could avalanche.

He found Lori talking to Reynolds at the back of the room, where the hallway led to the locker room. He could tell he was too late to make a difference. Reynolds was already berating Lori about something, looming over her with her large, rotund body to intimidate the younger and slimmer woman. God only knew what it was this time. He could tell from the look on Reynolds's face that she was angry, and she seemed to be telling Lori that it was her doing. When he approached them, he thought he saw a tear in Lori's eye as she turned away from him to hide her discomfort.

Reynolds was stating in her well-practiced, firm voice, "I'm not going to miss this important dinner with my husband's clients just because you can't herd these children onto the bus. I want you to get in there and get them moving now so that we can hit the road." She raised her voice. "Do you hear me?"

Lori looked completely cowed by the older woman. Her face was pale and distressed, and she was not her usual cheerful self. Her long blonde hair was tied back in a messy ponytail, and her blue eyes looked misty.

Reynolds turned to stare down Hardy as soon as he was close to them. "And I don't want to hear any more negativity from you, Mr. Harris. We are driving back to Durango just as soon as we can get the children on board that bus of yours. So I suggest that you pull it up out front so that we can leave right away. You hear me?"

"Mrs. Reynolds, be reasonable." Hardy had to try one more time to change what might be a horrible course of events. "It's starting to snow really hard outside. Look out the window! And if it's heavy down here in the valley, just imagine how it's snowing up on the mountains. And it's going to be dark in a half hour, so we'll have a hard time seeing the road once the snow accumulates." He looked back and forth between the two women. "It makes more sense to drive back on the long road through Cortez, where we won't have to fight through the heavy snow."

Reynolds had her arms across her chest in a defiant stance. Her brow was set, and her clipped, dark bangs seemed to amplify her stern position.

Hardy tried a new tactic. "It's either that, or we should stay here in Ouray overnight and drive back in the morning when the roads are clear."

Reynolds almost had a fit when he posed this last suggestion. "I just talked to my husband in Durango, and he said it wasn't even snowing there yet. You're getting all worked up about a local snowfall." She stepped back and put her hands on her hips. "You surprise me, Mr. Harris. I was told that you were a good driver for this trip, and now you seem to be afraid of shadows— not up to the job. I'll have to talk to my husband about whether you should be driving a school bus for the district. Maybe you aren't cut out for this job after all." She knew how to pull rank on anyone who worked for the school district—her husband's domain as a member of the Durango School Board.

Hardy knew that at sixty-seven, he was over the age that the district usually hired for a regular bus driver. If Mr. Reynolds wanted, he could have Hardy suspended any number of ways to keep his controlling wife satisfied. She knew the score, and so did Hardy. And he didn't want to get Lori Phillips in trouble since she had recommended him as a driver for the day, her attempt to get him some extra income that she knew he needed.

He decided then and there that he would have to drive over the pass, whether it made sense or not. He just hoped they could round up the kids and get moving as fast as possible.

"If that's your position, then I just want it known that I don't agree with you. The other way is safer." Hardy stated his opinion loud and clear to everyone in the room. He went on before Reynolds could cut him off.

"We need to get moving right now before the storm gets even worse." He then turned to Lori. "Where're the kids? In the locker room? I can go look for them, if you want."

Lori looked thankful that he would help her out. "Yes. They should all be getting dressed by now. I'll double check the pool area."

She fled Reynolds's presence. Hardy did the same, heading down the hall to the locker room.

He found only ten boys there, most of them still not dressed for the road. Hardy told them to get cracking because they were leaving in fifteen minutes. He asked where the other four boys were and was told that no one knew. He thought he had an idea of where a few of the slackers were and marched down the hallway to find the game room he had seen earlier. He rounded up two more boys there and got them moving toward the showers, encountering Lori in the hall with her son, Andrew, and his buddy Manny. When he saw that Lori had things in hand, he went outside to get the bus warmed up and ready to go.

Hardy waited out front as Lori and Mrs. Reynolds wrangled the Cub Scouts out of the distractions of the visitors center and herded them onto the bus. He had his best friend, Blue, with him on the bus, something that was not strictly regulation, but the boys all liked Old Blue, as they called him, an older and somewhat docile basset hound of some refined breeding and noble appearance.

Blue was a seven-year-old basset, tricolored, with brown, black, and white mixed in a pleasing pattern that left an oddly colored patch of grayish blue on his shoulders, resulting in his name. He loved children and was full of mischief when left unattended. He proved this today by knocking over his portable food dish, which his faithful master cleaned up before Mrs. Reynolds could see the mess. Blue's favorite place on the drive was on the seat next to one of the children, and he seemed to be especially taken by Andy Phillips, who he knew well. He often reclined next to anyone who would pet him and show him some attention, often draping his long ears on someone's lap and gazing up at them with his sad eyes in a sign of bonding.

Blue was Hardy's best listener, and he usually agreed with Hardy 100 percent. At least, that was what Hardy assumed.

The mobilization had taken nearly an hour, even though Hardy had made it clear they had to go *now!* He realized the kids were just having fun, and it was hard to get such a bunch of youngsters moving in the same direction at any speed, but he was worried. It was already as dark as could be after sunset, and the snow was coming down steadily, already more than two inches on the road. A final headcount confirmed that everyone was onboard; Martha was on her cell phone, telling her husband that they were on their way.

Hardy got moving up Highway 550 south, toward the steep winding canyon road. They climbed quickly at first, the tires of the school bus slicing their way through the snow and gripping the road underneath. The tires were in decent shape, but they were summer tires, even though Durango got its share of snow in winter. The fact was that none of the school buses for the Durango School District had winter tires because most of the bus routes ran at relatively low elevations where there wasn't much need for lugged gear. If a bus did get stuck on a wintry day, it was easy to call for a tow anywhere near the city. But today was different, and Hardy had thrown a set of tire chains in the toolbox on the bus just in case they needed them. He might be forced to put them on if things got slippery.

As they gained elevation on their way to the pass, the intensity of the storm increased to the point that it was difficult for Hardy to see the edges of the road. The centerline of the highway was under two to three inches of snow already, and the gravel verges of the road were completely cloaked in white. He had to guide the bus based on the reflective markers along the side of the road. He slowed down to keep centered in his lane—where he could see any lane at all. The thick, falling snow reflected his headlights back at him, increasing the difficulty of seeing the way. Occasionally they met an oncoming car or truck, headlights blazing, and the glare almost blinded Hardy.

One car came around a turn too fast and slid across the center of the road, nearly hitting the bus. The car didn't stop, but Hardy could see the fear in the other driver's eyes as he slipped past them. A few kids on the bus who saw what happened shrieked as the car went slipping by.

A semitrailer truck came down the mountain too fast as they crept up the grade, and Hardy had to pull over wide to the right and onto the gravel shoulder of the road to avoid a head-on crash. The truck didn't stop either, and maybe the driver couldn't, even if he wanted to. Hardy knew that the truck was an accident waiting to happen. This time everyone on the bus screamed as the big vehicle lurched onto the shoulder. He managed to maintain control of the bus but felt the rear wheels slip as he came back onto the asphalt; he shifted gears to keep the tires gripping the snow.

By now, they were driving through more than four inches of snow, with some ice underneath it, by the feel of the tires. He decided to stop at a turnout he knew of up ahead and put on the chains. He wasn't sure how they would make it without them.

"I'm going to pull over up here and put the chains on, OK?" he called out to all the passengers, especially Martha Reynolds. "It'll take a few minutes, but this is the only turnout before the pass. I could use some help if either of you ladies have ever put on chains before." He looked at the women in the rearview mirror, but only Lori had heard him. Martha was fiddling with her phone, trying to get a signal in this remote area but to no effect.

He looked around the bus to see how the kids were taking the idea of chains. No real fear had set in yet. That was a good thing.

He put on his heavy wool stocking cap, old winter parka, and leather gloves before stepping down the stairs and out the door. Old Blue leaped out and snorted when he got snow up his low-hanging nose. He snuffled the ground and then followed his master into the blizzard, his belly and long ears dragging in the powder. Blue was not as enamored with snow as many other dogs were. It was cold and wet, and he didn't like it when his ears got sodden from flopping around in the stuff.

Hardy was a no-nonsense kind of guy, getting up in years but in good shape due to his outdoor pastimes of hiking and camping. He had a weather-beaten face that was cheerful most of the time, even when beset by hardships or concerns. He had a moderate, graying mustache over his lip that became damp quickly in the cold weather as his breath condensed on it. He wore unstyled and uncut brown hair, also with a tint of gray in it that he usually tucked up under a Joe Eder Western hat, except today, when he sported a stocking cap. Sparkling brown eyes told you he was alert and capable. Apparently, all these qualities were lost on Martha Reynolds.

In a minute, Lori bundled herself up and came to help. They walked to the rear of the bus, and Hardy opened the back door to reach the chains in the toolbox on the floor behind the last row of seats. He assigned Lori the task of holding the flashlight so that he could see what he was doing, and they set about putting a chain on the right-side dual wheels.

The chains they had would fit over only one tire, so Hardy kicked the snow away from the wheel as much as possible with his boot, fitted the chain to the upper portion of the outer tire of the dual wheels, and then lay down next to the wheel to draw the rest of the chain around it. Then he got on the bus and backed up a foot or two to get the wheel onto the chain. Mrs. Reynolds barked at him. It took a while to get the chain stretched out right and the metal clamps to lock properly, but after about ten minutes, it was finished.

Then they moved to the other side of the bus to do the same there. That chain was missing a latch to lock it, and Hardy had to improvise with a piece of wire to keep the lock closed. By the time he had finished, he had taken off his gloves and was soaked from sweat and from getting snow down the back of his parka and up his sleeves.

Both Hardy and Lori were freezing by that time, with Lori shaking like crazy when they got back on the bus. Hardy helped his low-slung canine friend up the bus steps. They had barely stepped inside before Martha went on the warpath.

"What the devil took so long? We're just sitting here while you took your sweet time putting on chains. Look at how much time you spent—nearly half an hour. That's just not acceptable." She stamped her foot on the floor. "Now, let's get moving!"

As she shouted at Hardy, the boys stopped chattering. Some of them looked back and forth to see if their friends knew why Mrs. Reynolds was yelling at Hardy. They knew something was up. Blue gave a low woof in his master's defense.

Lori tried to object, but her courage caved as she faced Mrs. Reynolds's wicked stare. Hardy knew that it wasn't worth his breath to explain that they had had some trouble with the chains—old chains that he'd had the foresight to bring along, chains that they had put on because the bus did not have proper snow tires for winter driving. He turned away in disgust and belted himself into the driver's seat. He shifted into first gear and pulled back onto the road.

By now the storm had really intensified, and the wind was up, whipping and drifting snow across the road in a near whiteout. Hardy thought that maybe he should just turn the bus around and head back into Ouray, damn the consequences. But he knew that given the bus's length, he would not be able to turn around in the dark. And if he did, he would block the road. Anyone coming down the mountain wouldn't see him until it was too late, and the bus would get T-boned, smashed to pieces, and possibly pushed over the side of the road, down into the canyon and the river a thousand feet below.

He couldn't chance it. He had to press on into the pass and hope they could make it before the snows built up too deep for them to push through. Blue sensed that something was wrong and lay down next to Hardy as he drove.

Hardy realized that no one had come down from the pass the whole time they had been putting on the chains. What did that mean? Was there a problem on the other side of the pass that they didn't know about? Was there an accident ahead blocking the road?

He pressed on, gaining altitude and encountering more snow, nearly up to the axle, the chains biting into the snow and ice as they went. They entered the first portion of the pass. Hardy saw snow along the highway on the upslope side where loose snow from the slopes above had slid down the rocks in small cascades or sloughs, a little at a time, forming a sloping wedge of snow from the rock wall out onto the road. Some of the wedges reached a few feet into the upslope, inside lane of the road. He had to drive down the center of the road to avoid having the wheels dig through the extra snow.

In places, the snow was piled up in high banks on either side of the road. These were areas that had avalanched in the prior weeks—areas where snow on long slopes and in deep gullies above the road had slid down the mountain. Highway crews had cut a path through the slides, leaving eight-foot walls of snow on both sides of the road. No doubt, the current accumulating snow was building up in those same areas now, waiting until there was sufficient depth and weight to slide again. Hardy hurried past those stretches of the highway, eager to get to safer ground.

Hardy knew this stretch of road fairly well, having driven it many times for work and when exploring the outdoors in both summer and winter. He knew there were three main avalanche chutes to be concerned about, even though there were several places where smaller snow slides also crossed the road. The first one of the avalanche chutes was just ahead, and he drove through it with no problems.

The second chute was the biggest and most dangerous, closing the highway several times a year. It was so precarious that the state had built a huge concrete tunnel over that part of the road to protect drivers from the steepest area subject to avalanche. If he could get to that tunnel, he could pull the bus into it and wait for morning to arrive, keeping everyone safe under the protective concrete. He doubted that anyone else would be driving up here now that the storm was at full strength, which would explain the lack of any other traffic on the road. He thought that was the only reasonable thing to do now that they were here.

Hardy called to Lori and Mrs. Reynolds to come up front to talk about the storm while still plowing along the road in first gear at a snail's pace, pushing through a foot of snow or more. He told them what he was thinking.

"If we can make it to the tunnel," he said quietly so as not to scare the children, "we can wait there and be pretty safe until morning. If there's an avalanche down the chute above the tunnel, it'll mostly go over the top of us. In the morning someone'll come find us and dig us out. I don't think we have a cell phone signal up here, so we can't call anyone to let them know where we are, but people will realize something's wrong when we don't show up in Durango."

"I can't believe you'd give up so easily, Mr. Harris." Reynolds was the first to speak up. "Why, we're almost through this pass, as far as I can tell. There's no reason to stop up here in the wilderness overnight."

Lori was already scared and thought they should consider the idea. "I don't know, Martha. It sure seems to be coming down real hard out there. And there's so much snow, I don't know how Hardy can even stay on the road." Her eyes belied the fear that she felt. "Maybe we should pull over like he says."

"Well, I don't know about you, but I'm no quitter." Reynolds snorted. "No matter how difficult it is, I say we should keep going. We'll get through this in no time if Hardy would just step on it a little."

"Mrs. Reynolds, don't you get it?" Hardy raised his voice in anger, but he tried not to terrify the children. "This is dangerous out here, and we have a busload of kids to think about. Some of them seem pretty scared to me." He looked in the rearview mirror at the frightened faces of his young passengers. "I know I am."

As soon as he said that, he wished he hadn't. The kids closest to him had heard him say he was scared, and their eyes showed a new level of fear. Hardy was supposed to be the leader here, even if Martha Reynolds was technically in charge. He had to keep up appearances so that the kids wouldn't panic.

"Well, yes." Martha took up a defiant stance, arms akimbo. "Some of them are pretty scared, but they want to get home too. I think we've got to keep going. That's my position, and as the senior person here, that's what we'll do." Her mind was made up. "I don't want to let my husband down tonight."

Hardy started to protest, but she held up a hand like a traffic officer. She clenched her jaw to show her resolve. "Now, let's drive on. Remember that I'm in charge here, not you. You're just the bus driver." She set her jaw and stared at Hardy. "Now, drive!" Martha demanded loudly, a growl in her voice. She didn't care what the others said. She had to get home. She had her reasons.

The bus came around a turn and ran into a deep snowdrift that blocked the road.

"Oh shit!" Hardy mumbled under his breath as he quickly slammed on the brakes. The snowdrift was four feet deep and quite broad across the road. He put the bus in reverse and was able to back out of the drift, with much spinning of the chained rear wheels.

"OK, ladies. I'm going to go out there and see how much snow we have to push through. I'll be back in a minute." Hardy put on his parka, hat, and gloves and descended the steps at the door.

Blue tried to go with him but hesitated on the lowest step when he saw how deep the snow was. Then he leaped out and sank over his head. He started to follow Hardy and woofed for him to wait. Hardy saw the dog struggling in the deep powder.

"Hey, boy. You better sit this one out. You would need a snorkel out here. Go back on the bus."

Lori came down the steps and helped muscle Blue back inside, where she dried his paws on a towel, achieving Blue's greatest thanks, a slobbering tongue lick to the face and a wagging tail.

Hardy turned on his flashlight and waded into the deep drift in front of the bus. He was up to his waist in snow in no time, trying to determine how wide the drift was while holding the flashlight in one gloved hand and the other hand in front of his eyes so that he could see through the blowing snow. He went a little farther and saw that the drift was only thirty feet wide and two feet deep on the far side. They could probably push through it if he ran back and forth a few times with the bus, using it to break a path. He wondered what lay ahead and walked on to see around the next bend in the road.

He saw a light in the distance along the road, a single white glow that seemed to fade on and off as the wind blew snow his way in the night. He thought, *Thank God! It must be the light at the entrance of the tunnel.* They were closer to the tunnel and to safety than he had thought.

Hardy hurried back to the bus.

"OK. I saw the tunnel ahead." He looked down at the kids' faces. "Now, I want you all to sit down and hang on. We're going to have to ram our way through the snowdrift, and it might get bumpy."

With that, he revved up the engine and rushed forward into the drift. He plowed into it about six feet or so before he had to stop and back up. Then he rammed forward again even more. He backed up a second time and rammed ahead again until he thought he could break through with a final rush.

Hardy looked around at the terrified boys and a stubborn Mrs. Reynolds. "We're going to do it this time." He shouted, "Let's go, you old bus!"

He gunned the engine, the rear wheels spun, and the whole bus seemed to rise as they rode up and over the drift, a plume of snow thrown up by the rear wheels as they reached the other side. Some of the kids cheered when the bus broke free.

Now Hardy kept the bus's momentum up, and they drove steadily toward the tunnel. Everyone could see the light ahead now, and they all anticipated the safety it offered.

Some of the kids coaxed the bus along. "Come on, bus. You can do it!"

They closed the distance slowly, plowing through very deep snow now, the rear wheels spinning most of the time as they hit small drifts. They were only a hundred feet from the tunnel entrance, which they could now see through the snow, when they felt, rather than heard, a low rumble outside the bus. Hardy gunned the engine one last time as a wave of snow came rushing down the mountain out of the night and smacked the bus so hard that it bounced sideways toward the guardrail.

The bus held there for a half a second, then lifted up and went over the guardrail and off the side of the road into darkness as the avalanche swept them away.

***

Ouray County Sheriff's Deputy Eric Johansen came back to his patrol car through the steady, heavy snow with two cups of black coffee he had just purchased at Maggie's Kitchen. He handed one to the other deputy, Jorge "George" Garcia, who was riding shotgun. He climbed into the car, after taking off his utility belt with the holster on it, and placed the hot coffee in the cupholder.

He started the car and asked, "Hey, George, what are they sayin' about the weather?"

George sipped the hot brew before answering. "They say the storm is going to get a lot worse before it gets better. Like they always say." He chuckled as he smiled at Eric. "You know how it is. They can't really predict how these storms are going to happen; they just cover their bases with some mumbo jumbo statistics and hope they get close with a prediction. But the weather guy on the Grand Junction station made it sound like one of the really big ones." George was a pessimist when it came to believing any kind of radio news.

"How about road conditions?" Eric asked. "What's the word from the chief?"

"He said that we're to drive up to the snow gate and meet Tony Alvarez and Albert Kerty from the Ouray police there. We're closing the highway completely now. They did the same over at Silverton going this way up to the pass and going south over Molas Pass to Durango. We've also got 550 northbound closed at Purgatory Mountain just north of Durango. It's going to be a mess up in the passes tonight."

Eric listened to the radio again for a moment. "We better get goin'. There's some kind of problem up at the snow gate. Some trucker came down the mountain without chains on, and they're going to ticket him for that, so they need us to help out."

Eric had a hard time getting the Jeep Cherokee out of the parking space, spinning the rear wheels as he pulled into the southbound lane. He shifted into four-wheel drive, and the heavy cleats of the Firestone tires bit into the deepening snow.

They followed a plow truck along the streets to where the road left town. The snowplow pulled out to turn around since he was only doing the town streets. The snow gate was just a short distance ahead, and Eric and George saw the problem as they approached.

A semitrailer truck had apparently jackknifed when it tried to make the final turn into town, nearly hitting the other officer's patrol car, which was parked across the road at the gate. The truck was now blocking most of the road, and the driver was being harassed by the local cops for nearly hitting them and for violating the law regarding the required use of chains on the road in winter.

Eric and George went over to help their fellow policemen with the situation. Alvarez was shouting at the truck driver, asking him what kind of numbskull he was to not have his chains on. Kerty was writing up a ticket for the mandatory fine of $1,000 for running without chains under these conditions, a state law violation. Alvarez had the man get down and put his chains on the truck drive wheels now so that they could pull the semi out of the way.

Kerty came over to talk to the new arrivals.

"Hey, Eric! Hey, George! We got a real idiot over here. He said he just barely made it over the pass." He gave the trucker a severe stare. "He said it's real slick up there, and he didn't know it was going to be so bad when he started up the pass from Silverton two hours ago. He didn't think to stop and chain up. What an idiot!"

"Anybody else come through here lately? We closed the other end of the pass about an hour ago. How did this guy get through?" Eric asked as he surveyed the scene.

"We don't think anyone else got started up from the Silverton side because the Silverton police started turning people around earlier than we did here. We've only been here about forty-five minutes and stopped a few cars."

As they were talking, an incoming call came over Eric's radio. "Just a minute. Let me get that." He went to the car and reached in for the hand mic. He talked on the radio for a couple of minutes and then came back over to where the men were standing, including the somewhat upset truck driver.

"Hey, guys," Eric said with a troubled look on his face. "We just got a call from a Mr. Reynolds of the Durango School

District, asking where the hell his wife is." He smiled and held up his hand.

"I know what you're thinking, and I want to stop you right there, before you say something that will get you into trouble." The others muttered about bureaucrats. "He said she was here with a busload of Cub Scouts who came out to Ouray on a field trip, and they were supposed to start back to Durango an hour or more ago." He paused to let the news sink in. "Apparently his wife called him then and said they were just heading out. He wants to know if they were going to overnight here in Ouray now that the roads are closed." Eric looked at each of the other men's faces before continuing. "Has anyone seen a yellow school bus around town lately? It's Saturday, so it should be the only yellow bus drivin' around."

Alvarez spoke up first. "You know, I saw them about lunchtime over by the visitors center and pool. There were a bunch of kids. They had a den mother with them, a Lori something. I talked to her while I was getting coffee, and she said one of the boys was hers." He thought for a moment. "I'll call over to the center and ask when they left there." He walked to his patrol car to get his cell phone.

The truck driver was about to say something but then clammed up. He tried to pretend that he was just clearing his throat, but Eric noticed his behavior and thought it was odd. The driver looked guilty as hell, but Eric said nothing. The trucker was probably afraid he'd get in trouble if anything had happened to the bus. Maybe he thought he had better just get his truck on the road, take his ticket, and get the hell out of town fast.

Alvarez came back to the group. "I talked to Hatty at the visitors center, and she said the bus left here just after dark, say about five thirty. She said that the woman in charge had ordered the driver to take the pass even though he didn't want to. So they must have started up the mountain just before we got here at six."

Officer Kerty muttered as he stared at Alvarez. "We must have just missed 'em. They must be up there in the pass somewhere." He looked from face to face. "What the hell can we do? Go after them?"

George looked at Eric. "Can we contact them? Their cell phones probably won't work in the pass. They don't have radios on those school buses, do they?"

Eric thought about it a moment. "No. The husband said he had tried to call his wife and couldn't get through, just to voice mail. I really doubt that they have a radio on board the bus." Then he looked at Alvarez. "Tony, what's the situation here? Do you guys have this truck thing done already? Do you need us to stand by? We may have to go up to check on that bus."

"Yeah. Once this guy gets his rig out of the snow, we can guard the road just fine." He looked at the trucker and asked, "Say, you didn't see a school bus full of kids up there when you came through, did you? They would have been goin' up just about the time you were comin' through the pass."

The trucker looked like he had just been trapped in a vise. All the police officers noticed his behavior and knew he was holding back something.

"Hey, mister," Alvarez said. "If you know something and you don't tell us, you'll get in a lot of trouble, OK? So you'd better spit out whatever you know right now!"

"OK, OK," the trucker sputtered as he wiped his hand over his face. "Well, I did see a yellow bus go by up the hill, but they seemed to be moving along fine. It was up there just a little ways before that big turnout area this side of the pass, maybe ten or twelve miles up canyon. I had a hell of a time on the sharp turn there and had to swerve to avoid crossing the centerline. If that was them, they should have crossed the pass by now. But they were going real slow." He had his head down as he spoke, a sure sign that he was still holding back something.

"And what else?" Eric asked in a low, stern voice.

"Well," the trucker paused. "I can't be sure, but they seemed to be nearly off the road on the shoulder when I went by them."

"And you didn't stop to see if everything was all right?" Kerty was pretty upset that the man had just driven away without checking to see if the people on the bus were having trouble. "Were they OK?"

"Look, I was just barely able to keep my rig on the road myself. I couldn't have stopped if I wanted to. I hardly made it through that snow. I don't know how they could have been making progress at all in an old school bus."

Eric decided that they had to spring into action. "Look, you guys. George and I will contact the sheriff and start up the road after the bus. If they got stuck somewhere, we'll find them and radio for further assistance. If we can bring them back down, we'll help them do that. You guys call in and see what help you can pull together and coordinate with the sheriff, OK? We gotta get up there right away before things go to hell."

The trucker spoke up then in an attempt to help. "You boys had better put your chains on right now, 'cause you're goin' to need 'em. Must be over a foot of snow on the road already. Put chains on all your tires. Even that Jeep of yours will have a hell of a time with 'em on."

***

"That trucker wasn't kidding about the snow. We're just barely gettin' through this stuff," Eric said as the Jeep Cherokee struggled to pull itself through the deep snow, tire chains digging deep into powder on all four wheels.

They had been making slow progress up the highway, following the on-again, off-again trail that a large vehicle had left in the snow. In many places the tracks of what they thought must be the school bus were barely visible in the accumulating drifts. Now they approached a sizable snowdrift that blocked the road but that also showed signs of a vehicle passing.

"Look here, George," Eric said. "It seems like the bus must've come this far and pushed its way through. Maybe we can make it if we work a path back and forth."

George replied, "Yeah, if they went through, they may have packed the snow down a bit, and we can ride over some of it. Hang on!"

Eric rammed the Jeep into the drift and reversed back and forth several times, each time pushing farther along. Finally, they broke through and continued through deep snow, still following the ghost of a trail left by the bus. Then they encountered a huge mound of snow, a virtual wall of white and gray that buried the bus's tracks. They could continue no farther.

"Oh shit!" George blurted. "That's one big slide! We'd better back up out of here in case there's still some debris coming down the chute."

Eric reversed the Jeep a couple of hundred feet, hoping that would be enough to protect them from any following slide. With the wind swirling snow all around them, they could just barely see the main body of the avalanche at that distance. They could scarcely make out a trace of the tunnel beyond, its upper two feet or so still protruding above the snow and debris of the last slide.

Eric asked, "What d'you suppose happened? Did they make it into the tunnel? They get farther than that?"

"I don't know, Eric. I sure hope they made it through here before this avalanche hit. A big one like this could send the whole bus over the side or just bury them underneath tons of snow. You know how dense it can be in a slide like that."

"Shit," Eric said as he looked through the windshield as the blizzard raged all around them.

George was pretty nervous about sitting out there so close to the main avalanche chute in total darkness and in the midst of a swirling snowstorm. "I'm going to get out and look over the side of the road to see if I can see anything," he said. "Why don't you turn this rig around in the meantime?"

George took his Maglite flashlight and got out of the car. He was scared to death but knew he had to look for anything helpful related to the bus and what might have happened to it. He waded through deep snow to where he could see over the side of the road and looked downslope for anything unusual—like a school bus sticking out of the snow. He heard rocks and the sound of dense snow moving all around him, but he couldn't see more than fifty feet through the raging storm and moved back to the Jeep. Eric had finished turning the vehicle around.

George climbed back inside. "I can't see anything down there, but I really can't see very far at all with the snow comin' down. Let's get out of here. There's all kinds of stuff moving out there. It sounds like trees are snappin' and strainin' like the snow is shifting in the trees. I don't want to wind up under any of it."

They retraced their tracks back the way they came, unable to proceed forward any farther with the big avalanche across the highway. They drove nearly a mile to the location of the first big avalanche shoot in the pass. In their headlight view, they saw the remains of another large avalanche across the road that blocked their path. They had just crossed this same stretch of highway less than a half hour before, and now it was completely inundated with a gray jumble of ice and heavy, packed snow, chunks of wood and tree branches protruding from the massive pile of debris. They were trapped on the mountain, unable to drive back to Ouray or to go over the pass and down to Silverton.

"Well, shit!" Eric was more than a little agitated. "Now we're stuck up here for the night." He pounded his fists on the steering wheel in frustration. "We're lucky we got through here when we did, or we'd be buried alive. I'm going to drive back to that area with the snowdrift. It's out on a bit of a point, and we should be safe from any slides back there." He looked over at his partner. "Why don't you call in, George, and tell the sheriff what's happened."

Eric managed to turn the Jeep around, and they drove back to the big snowdrift to park for the night. The sheriff told them to get to a safe spot and wait for daylight. If the storm was done by then, the crews would begin plowing out the road from Ouray and probably from the Silverton side as well to clear the snow. He said the bus must be up there somewhere, but they couldn't risk sending anyone else out under the current conditions.

It was already eleven o'clock, and the storm kept up its fury as the men prepared to spend the night in their Jeep. They had winter survival supplies with them, as did most experienced mountain travelers. George had the sheriff call his wife and tell her that he was safe but stuck out for the night. Eric had no one in particular to notify. They settled in to await dawn.

***

Everyone was scared to death as the school bus lurched sideways and slid off the road in a sudden thunderous motion, into the blackness of the night and the raging storm. They were slammed against the side of the bus one moment and then thrown to the floor a few seconds later as the vehicle was tossed into the air before rolling over again and again. Then the bus stopped with a great crash, the left side down low and listing at a forty-five-degree angle.

Hardy was still belted into the driver's seat, but his head was banged up from hitting the side window and the steering wheel as the bus rolled over. He was conscious but confused by what had happened, and there was blood on the left side of his face. He had one hand firmly on the steering wheel and one hand on Old Blue, who was partway in his lap, as if he had flipped over and over with Hardy on the rolls. He had blood on his lower jaw. Blue looked at Hardy for some indication of what had just happened.

It was very quiet on the bus—too quiet.

When Hardy came to his senses, he realized that it wasn't quiet at all. Children began to cry out, and some whimpered in fear. He shook off the last of the daze he was in, unbelted himself, and set Blue on the floor. Then he turned and was surprised to find that the bus's dome lighting was still working, giving the interior a faint orange glow. He saw kids strewn everywhere, some up against the left side of the bus and others folded onto the bus seats. One or two looked like they hadn't moved at all during the ordeal.

He looked for Lori and saw her at the back of the bus, moving slowly and trying to help one of the boys. He saw Reynolds lurched to the side of the bus in an awkward, nearly upside-down position, trying to right herself.

Hardy moved down the aisle of the bus, checking on everyone as he went, pulling them up into a sitting position on the steeply sloping seats and seeing how badly banged up each one was. He helped the kids first, but when he came to Martha, he had to stop and pull her into a sitting position. She wasn't able to keep herself upright and had blood in her hair.

The kids seemed to have just rolled around in the spinning bus like they were in a washing machine, and they did not appear to have any serious injuries. He reached Lori and found her sitting up and holding on to one of the boys, who was crying into her chest out of plain fear. Blood ran down Lori's face from a cut on her forehead, but she appeared alert and in control of her emotions, something mothers always seem to be able to do when children are in danger.

Somehow they were all still alive. Then the bus moved a little, and gasps of fear echoed through the metal vehicle. But it only settled into a slightly different position and then stopped.

Lori looked up at Hardy with terror in her eyes. Andy, her son, came up to her and hugged her tightly for protection. "Hardy, what happened?"

Hardy answered her as best he could. "We were pushed off the road by an avalanche, I think. But the bus is still in pretty good shape, not crushed or anything like you'd expect." Then he stopped talking. He needed to see just what the hell had happened. He had no idea where they were. *Hell, maybe they were still in danger.*

But first things first. Here he was jabbering, and Lori, Martha, and maybe others were bleeding. He rushed forward along the sloping aisle to where the first aid kit was lashed to the wall of the bus. He got it and came back to Lori, whose injury was now bleeding heavily. He pulled out a sterile compress to put on her forehead to stop the flow. He checked that it was not a deep wound and then used adhesive tape to hold the compress in place.

"I need help! I need help!" Martha suddenly woke from her personal daze in a frenzy of fear. "Oh my God! I'm bleeding! Get over here with some bandages, you foolish man. I need help."

Hardy was about to explode with rage at her selfish demand when Lori intervened. "I'll take care of Martha and the others, Hardy. Why don't you do whatever is necessary to get us out of here." She took the first aid kit from his hands and shuffled up to where Martha was having her hysterics.

As Hardy moved past Martha, he gave her the evil eye on his way to the front of the bus. He looked over the vehicle's interior, noticing that the windows on the left, or downhill, side had all been cracked badly, but being safety glass, they had not broken in, preventing snow from entering the vehicle. Most of the other windows were in the same condition, with only two actually broken out of their frames. The body of the bus was bent in the middle, and the whole roof was smashed down a few inches, but the sides were not badly deformed.

He still wore his coat and hat from his earlier snowdrift exploits, found his gloves, and shuffled to the bus door. With the bus listing the way it was, he had to climb up to the doorway by clinging to the steps. Then it occurred to him that the door might be jammed or that snow might pour into the bus when he opened it. Using his flashlight beam, he was pleased to see that there was snow only partially up the door on the outside. He unlatched the door, which jammed partway open. He worked one panel until it was wide enough to crawl through; once outside, he could he could stand up and look around.

He stepped out onto the broken boughs of a spruce tree, which had apparently stopped the bus midslope. The trunk of the tree was under the bus and held it up in the steep forty-five-degree angle, so the frame had taken most of the impact as the bus hit the tree. He realized that if they had hit the tree in a different orientation, say roof-first, the whole cabin of the bus would probably have been crushed. They had been extremely lucky.

Hardy climbed up higher to push past the branch for a better look around, but all he could see beyond the tree was darkness and blowing snow. Although his view was limited, he could sense the great void that lay out there, the steep slope and an abyss below them.

When he looked back along the right side of the bus, he saw that most of it was clear of snow other than a light layer of newly fallen powder. The front of the bus was buried as far as he could tell. He crawled out farther to look over the top of the bus and saw that the left side and much of the top were completely buried under avalanche debris and the snow-ice mixture that results from snow sliding down the mountainside. Then he crawled down to look under the chassis and saw that the tree had indeed stopped them where they were, but it was almost torn in half and had less packed debris underneath.

It looked like the bus could still settle more if they ran out of luck. *Oh God*, he thought. *Just give us a little more good fortune, and we may get through this.*

Hardy came back inside the bus and was relieved to know they were not going to slide down the slope more unless conditions changed dramatically. He told everyone they were safe for now and went from seat to seat to see how the kids were doing. Lori said there were only two severe injuries. One boy had a broken arm, and one had twisted his leg badly during the crash. Mrs. Reynolds was somewhat subdued now that she realized she was not dramatically injured. Lori managed to get her to help comfort some of the boys.

Hardy looked at his watch and was surprised to see that it was already midnight. He addressed the passengers.

"OK, everyone. We were knocked off the road by an avalanche and are stuck on the side of the mountain because a big tree happened to stop us here. We were lucky!" He scanned the upturned faces, some on the verge of tears, all of them as scared as could be.

"Hardy," Lori asked quietly, "what do we do?"

"We'll be OK, I think." He looked at her and gave her a reassuring glance before continuing to address the others. "But there's nothing we can do right now because it's still snowing hard, and it's too dark to see anything at all. We're going to have to wait here until daylight and maybe even longer until help reaches us."

He looked around to assess how terrified the boys were. Some seemed really scared, and some were already acting like it was an adventure, something to talk about when they got home. He looked at Lori and then at Martha.

He spoke directly to the boys. "I can keep the dome light on for most of the night, I think, and we also have flashlights if the bus's battery runs down. So we should be all right here through the night. Now I'll let Mrs. Reynolds and Mrs. Phillips tell you what the situation is for food, drink, and sleeping conditions, OK?" He tried to give the kids a reassuring smile and then swiveled his head to look at Lori's solemn face.

Hardy went up front to check on the engine and battery status while Reynolds took charge of the troops. Of course, her idea of being in charge was to blame Hardy for getting them stuck on the mountain. The kids knew better, and she soon realized they weren't buying her story. She sat down.

Lori then took over and made the kids comfortable for the night, after distributing cookies and juice packs all around. She even gave Martha her own share so that the woman would stop complaining about missing the important dinner with her husband and his associates. Hardy was content to drink coffee from his stainless steel thermos that he had replenished at the visitors center before they left Ouray.

Hardy made sure the electric heaters that had been installed for winter use were working. They would help keep the air temperature on the bus from dropping below about fifty degrees if the separate batteries were fully charged. He helped distribute wool blankets for the kids to wrap up in and get them settled along the floor of the bus. Even the adults managed to stretch out for the night. Hardy had Blue wrapped up in his blanket to keep them both warm. Before long, everyone fell asleep from exhaustion.

***

Halfway through the night, Eric woke up and had to answer the call of nature. He put on his coat and hat and stepped outside. The wind had calmed down a little by that time, and the rate of snowfall had decreased substantially. He stood along the side of the road and looked out over the valley below.

While standing there, he noticed several strange noises coming from the slope above them and over by the large avalanche chute and tunnel. He heard the sound of shifting snow and saw some small, white sloughs coming down the mountainside behind him. Then he heard some rocks come bouncing down the chute, small stuff mostly, with what sounded like minor snow slides accompanying them. He wondered if the chute would release another avalanche tonight. If so, he hoped it stayed in the same track and followed the first one down into the valley two thousand feet below.

He went back to the Jeep and tried to sleep again. It was hard to do so as he thought about those poor people out there in the storm somewhere, most likely stuck, cold, and afraid. He wondered what it must be like for the parents of the Cub Scouts, worried sick about them, not knowing where they were or if they were safe. He looked over at George, who was sleeping like a champ, his family safe at home. He would see them tomorrow.

Then he wondered what was going through the bus driver's mind. He must have known it wasn't safe to start up here on such a crazy night. But Eric had already heard that the man was ordered to drive by the woman who seemed to be in charge. At least, that's what Hatty had told Alvarez. Eric had talked to the driver, this guy, Hardy, before and thought he was OK and had his head on right. He wouldn't want to be in his shoes now.

No, sir. Not tonight.

***

Hardy couldn't sleep worth a damn. He had drifted off at first because he was worn out by the stress of it all. Then he woke up about two in the morning when a large slough of snow slid down the slope and piled up against the roof of the bus. This seemed to happen every half hour or so as snow gathering on the slope above them built up and then slid down all of a sudden. They weren't big slides, but they shook the bus when they hit.

Hardy crawled outside to look at the snow around the bus and was surprised to see that the snow from the sloughs had built up to cover the entire roof. Any new sloughs were passing over the bus on their way downslope. On the one hand, it was good to see the snow pass over them and not bury them, but at the same time, the extra weight caused the bus to shift.

Now some of the snow coming down the slope was piling up against the bus's front door, making it hard to open without a pile of snow coming in. He noticed that the tree holding them in position moved a little as the snow built up. If it gave way, the bus would be dislodged and tumble down the slope wildly.

Hardy shook his head. "We're screwed," he muttered to himself. "Can't do anything about it till daybreak."

He crawled back inside and tried to shut out the snow as well as he could. Now a little ramp of snow had built up inside the door so that he and Blue had to move farther back from the door to avoid it. As he repositioned their bedding, he noticed that Lori and Martha were also awake near the back of the bus. He shuffled their way to see how they were feeling.

He shined the flashlight on them a second to see how they were situated and noticed that Lori was very pale. She was wrapped up in a blanket with her boy, Andy, who was asleep.

Hardy went to them, lifted her bandage, and was surprised to see that the wound was still bleeding, even though he had redressed it before they all turned in for the night. She seemed very groggy, which was not an encouraging sign, and fell back to sleep immediately. He asked Martha if she had noticed the bleeding.

"Why, no. I was just scrunched up here, minding my own business and trying to sleep. She didn't say anything, so I assumed she was asleep." Martha was a bit indignant that she had not noticed something was wrong. "Is she OK?"

"Martha, I don't know for sure, but with a head wound, we have to worry about blood loss and a possible concussion. I'm going to redress her wound again and wake her up for it. Then we'll see how she feels."

Hardy woke Lori again and asked her a few simple questions. She could just barely answer, which seemed beyond the confusion he expected from someone who was just tired. He spent some time pulling the wound together with several butterfly bandages from the kit, then put a dressing over the entire area and taped it up. That seemed to stop the bleeding for now. He was worried about her being so out of it mentally. *There must be a concussion too*, he thought. *That's really bad news.*

"Martha, I want you to keep an eye on Lori for me. She's in trouble." He scratched his chin as he spoke. "It's a concussion, I think. That's serious. She should get to a doctor right away. I need you to talk to her for a while and then see if you can wake her once every hour or so to be sure she doesn't go out too deeply. Can you do that?" He gave the irritating woman a hard stare that appeared to get her attention. "Just talk to her about anything to keep her mind partly occupied. OK?"

Then Hardy examined Martha's head wound, which looked pretty good. "You'll be all right, Martha. The bleeding has stopped, and you have normal color in your face."

He then moved to check on the kids, one by one, waking them momentarily to be sure they were OK. They were wrapped up in pairs to keep each other warm in the blankets. They seemed to be sleeping well. Hardy wondered why adults lost the ability to completely conk out like that when older. *We must all have too much to worry about nowadays*, he thought.

Hardy went back to where Blue was keeping the blanket warm and wrapped himself next to the hound. He couldn't sleep as his mind wandered over all the worst-case scenarios. He was worried that if the bus was so badly covered with snow, the road crews wouldn't be able to find them when they finally made it up the pass. He had to come up with a plan to either crawl up to the road or make some kind of flag to wave to get someone's attention. It bothered him that he didn't even know how far down the slope they had slid. But he couldn't do anything until he had daylight on his side.

Then he started thinking that he should have stood up to Martha in the first place and not let her force his hand like she had. If he had refused to drive, they wouldn't be in this mess. He and Blue would either be sleeping in a hotel room in Ouray or they would be home after a long drive through Cortez.

"Yes, I should have stood up to her, Blue," he whispered to his furry companion. "I should have held my ground."

In the old days, he would have thought nothing of making a stand like that, regardless of the consequences. But these days he seemed to be less certain of things, less sure of what he was doing. If he didn't have Old Blue, he wouldn't have a good reason to get up in the morning some days. *Life isn't as much fun as it used to be.* And he missed Lily. He *really* missed Lily.

Hardy felt a heavy weight come over his being as he laid there, one arm around Blue and one pulling the blanket around him. It had been three years now since Lily had died unexpectedly of cancer. They had been really happy right up until she started having pains in her belly. *Cancer of the pancreas* the doctor said.

They came up with all sorts of possible treatments, which all sounded awful, and the doctors had given her only a few months. In the end, Lily decided they couldn't afford any of it, and she didn't want to go through all that pain just to drag out the act of dying. She said she knew he couldn't stand to be there every day and watch her endure that. And she didn't want to inflict that on the only man she had ever really loved in her life.

He had tried to argue with her, but it was settled. She hung on ten weeks and then Hardy was alone.

He cried there in the dark, wondering what was coming over him. He couldn't break down, not in front of all these kids. *Marines don't cry*, he thought. *We stick together and fight on.*

He was alone.

Well, he had Old Blue, and that was something. Hardy found him at a rescue shelter a few months after he had lost Lily, looking forlorn and unloved, so they joined forces and had been great friends ever since.

Then Hardy realized that Blue was licking the side of his face, telling him in his way that it was going to be all right. He looked down at his best friend and mumbled, "Well, at least you've got my back, don't you, old boy?" He patted him on the head and scratched his ears where he liked it.

Then he thought about how happy he and Lily had been when they first came to Colorado from South Dakota nearly two decades ago. Lily had wanted to live in the mountains and found a teaching job at one of the schools in Durango, so there they settled. They didn't have a lot after he left the Marine Corps and San Diego to go home to Pierre. They had only a little more when they came west to Colorado, but they made ends meet. He got a job as a mechanic for a while and then worked at a hardware store, picking up the school bus driving job later. Now that was his main job with some part-time work at the hardware store and a gun shop on the edge of town. His retirement barely covered the cost of his simple way of life, but he was OK.

Maybe that was why the threat Reynolds made about him losing his job had scared him so much. If he didn't drive a bus, he didn't know what he would do. It wasn't just the money. He really enjoyed seeing all the kids every morning. It gave him something to look forward to. And they seemed to like him too. That's how he met Lori and Andrew, through Lily and the bus. Lily had helped Lori with a few things around the house when she, Hardy, and Lily became friends. After Lori's husband died, they were there to help as they could. Lori had a hard time raising Andy alone, and Hardy had stepped in to take the boy fishing a couple of times and even drove to a few ball games in Denver. *Nice kid, that Andy.* Then when Lily died—*yes, when she died* . . . The thought came over him like a heavy, wet blanket, taking his breath away for a moment. Lori had taken charge of him for dinners once in a while. Soon the three of them were often together.

But here he was a broken-down old man with just an aging dog to show for all his life of livin'. Maybe Martha was right and he was too old and unsure of himself to be driving a school bus.

Maybe I'm all washed up. He couldn't imagine that the school board would let him keep driving after this fiasco. What would happen? He checked his watch. It was five in the morning, just two hours to sunup.

***

Martha sat in the dark next to Lori and Andy, wondering if she should be as terrified as she felt. She tried to control her fear but was afraid that if she let go of herself even a little, she would break down in an embarrassing spasm of emotion. She had one boy sleeping with her, a Tommy something. She wasn't quite sure of his last name, and that surprised her since she made it a point to remember people's names. *It must be the situation*, she thought.

Ever since she had married Roger, a rising star in the local Republican Party, she had trained herself to be the perfect political wife. And that meant taking charge of things at home and on the road, remembering names and other details of anyone her husband considered important in his position and career. But lately, she felt she had been slipping somehow. She was beginning to forget names and details, and it worried her. And her split-second wit and decision-making ability were beginning to fail.

Then there was this trip today. She had come along because Lori Phillips, a woman very popular at school and who was friends with some people that Roger liked, had needed someone to help her with the large group of Cub Scouts. She had convinced Martha, playing on Martha's weakness that she *sure* was a good organizer, and her son had been a Cubby once. And Martha had wanted to see an old friend in Ouray anyway, so it worked out. But she should never have done it on a day when Roger had invited the Marchants over for dinner.

She thought she could do the trip and be back in time for dinner but then everything went to hell. The trip had started late, the boys took much too long in the pool, and then this dreadful snowstorm had begun. And she had made a scene about driving through it.

What had come over me? I'm not thinking clearly anymore. It seemed like every once in a while, she said or did things she thought better of afterward. But it was usually too late then. And she had become a bully sometimes. She didn't know why, but sometimes she felt desperate.

Like today, she thought. She had suddenly panicked that she would let Roger down if she didn't get back and make the dinner a success. It was like a cloud of fear came over her. She sat there quietly, hugging little Tommy, and a tear formed in her eye. She had yelled at Lori and blamed her for running late, something she had little control over. After all, they had picked Martha up at her house as a favor to save her any driving, and that was why they were behind to begin with. She really liked Lori and hoped that she could make it up to her.

And why was I so mean to Hardy? He was one of the nicest men she knew, if a little rumpled and down on his luck, but that wasn't his fault. He just wasn't the kind of person she was used to dealing with in her role as a political wife. Why was she so tense? Why did she take it out on others? And, more important, what was it that had her so afraid?

Martha realized that Lori was looking at her, more lucid than she'd been all night, her eyes open and with a look of understanding on her face. "Sorry, Martha. But you were talking to yourself, and I couldn't help hearing the last part. Why is this dinner for Roger so important tonight? It's got you worked up like I've never seen you before. What's the matter?"

Martha stiffened when she realized she had been muttering her thoughts out loud. She liked Lori but wasn't sure how much she should say to her. "Well, it's just that the Marchants are very important people in the party, and, you know, Roger is getting ready to step up and maybe try to run for the state legislature next year." She hesitated. "The Marchants would be good to have on his side. But I feel like I've let him down tonight. I should have been there to support him and remind him of important things. You know, the little things you do to help your husband like that."

Then Martha inhaled deeply. "Oh, I'm sorry." She felt ashamed. *There, I did it again*, she thought. She continued. "I forgot about your husband being gone. It must be hard to be alone, with little Andy and all. I don't know what I would do if I lost Roger or if he left me. I'd . . ." She stopped dead, mortified at the thought, and looked at Lori. She began to cry quietly.

Lori wondered about the other woman's comment. "What do you mean, Martha? Aren't you and Roger getting along?" She gave Martha a sympathetic smile. "Oh dear. No wonder you're so upset all the time."

"I don't know, but it's hard. With Roger's career about to take off on a statewide stage, we've been talking about moving to Denver. Will he still need me when we get there?"

She looked at Lori through her tears and cried quietly. "I don't want to leave our little town of Durango. I like it here in the mountains. I'd miss all the nice people. People like you and the other friends we've made over the years." She looked at Lori and burst into deep sobs.

Lori reached out and pulled the desolate woman over to her and let her rest her head on her shoulder, the one that Andy did not already occupy. She comforted Martha as best she could for a time. Then she fell into a deep sleep, holding two frightened people to her.

***

Hardy woke up shortly after it turned to daylight. The snowstorm was slowing down significantly, and the light that came in from the few windows that were not buried gave him hope. Even Blue seemed energized by the dawn. He licked Hardy's face and struggled to unwind himself from the blanket. He needed to go outside in a big way.

Hardy crawled up from the angled position the two had been in all night and felt like he had been in some sort of cage fight, aching all over. He stood up as much as possible in the confined space and stretched. He looked at the rest of the occupants of the bus hotel and saw no movement. *Might as well let them sleep, if they can,* he thought. *Blue and me, we can take a look outside.*

He went to the front of the bus and opened the folding door. Blue climbed the ramp of snow and stepped out onto fairly dense powder that let him shuffle a few feet over to a nearby branch that he then watered with a look of relief. Hardy tested the snow to see if it would support his weight and found he sank only a few inches. But he was wary that he could break through at any time. He looked down the slope and made use of the same branch that Blue had initiated.

He could see much farther now than he could last night in the heavy snowfall and dim illumination of the flashlight. He could peer far down into the valley, but the bottom still eluded him.

Looking up, all he saw was a snow slope, the dark gray chute of the avalanche track that had caught them unaware last night. It was now covered with the remnants of snow and slough that had slid down as they slept. He could see a black patch of rock projecting above him and wondered if that could be part of the road cut of the highway. It wasn't so far away above him, about two or three hundred feet. Maybe he could climb up there and see if there was any hope of a road nearby.

He decided to give it a try and told Old Blue to stay with the bus while he made an attempt to climb up the hard-packed snow slope. He started out well, kicking his boots into the snow with care to be sure he had a firm foothold before putting his full weight on each step. He got up about fifty feet above the bus when he encountered lots of branches in the snow and an icy hardness on the surface. He couldn't kick steps into the frozen surface, so he tried to use the buried pieces of wood and branches for support. That seemed to work, so he gently held on to anything else he could reach to help him. Blue watched his every move, occasionally commenting with a low woof from the door of the bus.

He made it up about seventy feet before a piece of wood he grabbed onto came out of the snow, and he went over backward. *Oh shit!* was all he thought as he fell and began to slide downslope on his back, headfirst and picking up speed.

He had a piece of wood in his hand, and he stuck it in the snow at his side as he slid. It dug into the softer powder, and he managed to turn around to travel feetfirst. As he slid by the bus, he heard Blue barking loudly. Hardy knew he had to get onto his belly so that he could use his hands to dig into the snow. He twisted sideways and flipped over. Then he hit a branch with his foot that nearly flipped him backward again. Finally, he ran into a patch of softer snow, and he dug his fingers and feet in to stop.

He was fifty feet below the bus. Blue was looking at him, ready to jump down the slope to help.

Hardy lay there on his belly, his hands dug into the soft slough, and tried to catch his breath, panting hard and scared into silence. But he realized that Blue was going to attempt a rescue, and he knew the dog had no chance of balancing on this hard layer of winter whiteness.

"Stay there, Blue. Good boy! Stay!" he called. "Don't try to come down here. Sit down, boy! Sit!"

Sit was one of the few real commands that Blue believed in because it usually meant a treat was following. That seemed to work, and the combination of the commands to sit and stay, along with Blue's fear of sliding on snow, kept him on the bus.

Suddenly a head appeared next to Blue's. It was Martha, looking around and finally down to where Hardy lay sprawled out on the snow. She panicked when she saw him.

"Hardy! Hardy! Are you all right?" she shrieked. "What in blazes are you doing down there?"

"Martha, I was trying to go up the slope but fell. Can you look for the safety rope behind the driver's seat?" He hoped the rope was where it was supposed to be after the crash. "If you can find it, tie one end to the leg of the driver's seat and lower the other end to me, OK?"

He hoped Martha would hurry. She disappeared inside the bus. Blue kept vigil at the door, now bellowing in a deep basset baritone characteristic of the breed.

Baroo! Baroo! Baroo! His bark echoed across the valley.

In a minute or two, Andy's head appeared, and he threw the free end of the rope down the slope to Hardy, dropping it right in his hands. Hardy pulled hard on the rope a few times, glad that he had a bus full of Cub Scouts who could tie knots. He slowly climbed up the slope, now holding on to the rope with his hands and kicking his feet into the snow. As he did so, various scouts stuck their heads out of the bus in turns to watch Hardy climb up the slope. Then Martha reappeared, and she reached out to grab the arm of his jacket as he struggled onto the bus.

"My God, Hardy! Look at your hands." Only then did Hardy begin to feel pain from the cuts, scrapes, and bruises his hands had suffered as he'd flailed for anything to hold on to during his slide down the snow. Blue pushed his way over to him and licked his hands in eager greeting.

Hardy had barely gotten into the bus before Andy reappeared, eyes wide with fear. "Hardy, come quick! Mom won't wake up. I tried to shake her and everything, but she just doesn't open her eyes." The boy gave him a pleading stare. "You've gotta help her!"

He scrambled to the back of the bus.

Hardy had just begun to think that he had the right to feel a little bit sorry for himself, but he cast those thoughts aside and followed Andy. Lori lay curled up in the blanket, unconscious and very pale. Hardy touched her forehead with the back of his hand. It was warm. Then he searched for a pulse at the side of her neck. He felt a weak beat there, but his hands were torn up pretty bad, and he wasn't sure. He put his head low beside her head and listened for breath. Yes! She was breathing, but just barely.

He had Andy fetch him the first aid kit and checked her dressing, but it seemed that the bleeding had stopped. He found some smelling salts inside the kit and popped a capsule under Lori's nose. She responded weakly, opening her eyes briefly and breathing in deeply. She mumbled something and reached out for Andy, hugging him for a few moments before she gradually lapsed into darkness again.

Hardy looked at Lori, then at Andy, clinging dearly to his mom. He and Reynolds moved Lori so that she lay flat on the floor where she could breathe easier and then they went to the front of the bus to talk. "Martha, we have to get her help real soon. I don't know what's the matter with her, but I know she needs emergency care. She may be bleeding internally and might have a concussion. We have to get the hell out of here."

Hardy realized that Old Blue was on the top of the snow slope outside the door of the bus, bellowing into the light snowfall for help in his own way. *Baroo! Baroo!*

Hardy joined him and shouted too. "Help! Help!" Then: *Baroo! Baroo!*

Maybe a miracle will happen, he thought, *and someone will hear us in the middle of nowhere.*

***

High up on the avalanche chute, the heavy snowfall from the last eighteen hours was beginning to settle in the weak early-morning sun. It was shifting under its own weight, and the sun was causing some of it to melt just a little—enough to cause it to slip on the rocks underneath. The portion of the chute that had broken loose last evening had roared and rumbled down the mountain in unconstrained fury to cross the highway. But higher up the mountain, near the head of the chute, there was a huge basin that funneled down the rest of the way and that was now covered in a thick layer of new snow. It had not broken loose during the night and was overdue for a slide—a big one. The snow shifted a little and then the pressure concentrated more and more as the snow continued to fall up high, the sun filtered through, and the temperature began to rise.

***

Eric was on the radio just after dawn. He contacted the sheriff's office to see what was happening down in Ouray, far below the wintery perch where they had spent the night in the patrol car. He learned that a full-scale search and rescue effort had been organized to look for the school bus and another car that was unaccounted for. People were assembling for a desperate search in Ouray, Silverton, and Durango. The problem was that the snowstorm had been intense most of the night, leaving a foot of snow in the valleys but several feet of powder in the higher elevations, making highway travel virtually impossible until the roads were plowed out. Road crews were already at work in all the towns, and they were heading up Highway 550 from Ouray with trucks and front-end loaders, but the snow was heavy and slow to remove.

The sheriff's department had sent out a full-size tracked snowcat, a vehicle that had wide tracks instead of tires, allowing it to drive on top of the snow. Two deputies were driving the cat up the highway ahead of the snowplows to see how bad conditions were. Eric reported that things were just beginning to improve up on the mountain, the storm lessening in the morning light.

As he signed off, George knocked on the outside of the car window. Eric got out to see what he wanted. They had repositioned close to the big avalanche track they had found the night before. It looked like there had been a series of small snow slides overnight on top of the first avalanche and along its sides.

"Hey, Eric! Look down that slope there. I heard a coyote or something howling and thought I saw it on the slope, but I can't make it out. Here, you take a look." He handed Eric the binoculars and pointed down the mountainside.

First, Eric looked around to see how much the light had improved, now that the snow was letting up. He looked downslope and saw nothing but white and a few patches of brush. He didn't see anything like a coyote or an animal of any kind. However, he did hear a low rolling sound from somewhere down below them. It might have been a howl. But he also heard a sound above them that caught his and George's attention, a high-pitched screech that told them that trees were rubbing against each other, wood on wood. That often indicated that snow was moving slowly and bending trees.

"Shit, George!" Eric lowered the binos and looked up the avalanche chute. "It sounds like there's more snow getting ready to cut loose up there. I hope it's not right over us."

"Yeah, no shit! Maybe we should move back to the place where we spent the night. It was safer there."

Baroo! Baroo! The sound came to them weakly on the wind, a low tone from below. Eric looked down the slope again, scouring it for signs of a coyote, but saw nothing. Then a gust of wind blew the snowfall aside for a moment, and he glimpsed movement on the slope not too far away. Then he lost it. *Baroo!* He saw a flash of something again. *A coyote?* he thought. *Maybe buried deep in snow?* He refocused the lenses and strained his eyes to see through the snow. It moved again, raising its head to howl. A big head with long ears.

"Hell, George! That's not a coyote! It's a dog." He glanced at George to see if his partner saw what he was seeing. "It's Hardy's old basset hound standing out there on the avalanche!" Eric finally saw Old Blue through the binoculars. "They must be down there! Here, you look. I'm going to honk the car horn. See if the dog responds."

***

Hardy couldn't keep up the yelling. His voice began to give out soon enough. He sat there just inside the doorway, out of the snow, and let Blue sing out his woes in a type of prehistoric call of the wild that only he could understand. One thing Blue was really good at was howling, and now was no time for him to let up. He had a lot of angst and worry to project into the valley, and the song echoed back to him from all around them.

Hardy looked around the inside of the bus at the scouts and the two women, only one now trying to keep the kids from fear, even though she, Martha, was just barely holding down her own panic. What a dismal situation they were in. But he had been in worse ones and had never given up hope.

Then Hardy's ear caught a new sound. A car horn? How in the world could that be? No one was up there in the middle of nowhere.

Beep! Beep!

That's a horn, he thought, *but where is it coming from?* He stuck his head out the door to hear better. *I'll be damned. It is a horn!* He looked up the slope through the falling snow. *Did I just see something move up there?*

He stood up in the doorway, holding on to the door handle, and waved his free arm in big arcing motions to get someone's—anyone's—attention. "Hello! Hello!" he called. Then he saw a man waving back at him. Hardy could just barely make him out. Then the storm picked up again, and he lost sight of anything except snowflakes.

He kept waving his arm, wondering if he should tell the kids that maybe someone was up on the road above them, but he wasn't sure if he should get their hopes up too soon. He didn't realize he had been thinking about it for so long until he heard someone call to him. "Hello! Hardy, are you there?"

He looked outside again and saw one of the deputies he had met in Ouray yesterday coming down the slope on a diagonal toward the bus. He was tied onto a rope and was fighting his way over to them, struggling against the rope because it was anchored over to the right of the bus, up high somewhere. He made it to the door, and Hardy grabbed his hand, pulling him inside.

"Hi! I'm Eric with the Ouray County Sheriff's Department." He looked at all the scout faces and said, "Who wants to get out of here?"

The busload of kids shouted back at him and cheered.

Hardy explained that they had an injured woman and that they had to get her to a doctor fast. Eric went over to Lori and verified what Hardy told him. Then he checked on the kids and Martha and walked back to talk to Hardy.

"OK, Hardy. I have a plan to get you all up to the road, but it will take a lot of teamwork." Eric looked around at the boys. "I'm going back to the road to get ready. I have two climbing ropes in the car that we use for mountain rescue. I had to tie two together to come down here. You're a little over two hundred feet below the road, almost three hundred feet on the diagonal. It's a real miracle that the bus landed here. I don't want to scare you, but on the way down, I noticed that you're only a hundred feet or so above a cliff, just off to the side of the main avalanche chute."

He looked at the kids before directing his attention to Hardy again. "I'll head back so that George and I can get things rigged up. Then we'll start pulling you folks up, one at a time, to the road. I think we can run the cable from the winch on the front of our Jeep down here, and we can hook it up to the doorframe here." He slapped the metal handle next to the door, the one people use when climbing up the stairs of the bus. "We'll use that as a guideline that each person will hook onto with a carabiner." He paused. "You know, one of those aluminum climbing links. You can hook each kid to the cable, then tie them onto the rope. Then we can pull them up on the rope. We have a couple of climbing harnesses like this in the car." He pointed to the harness he had around his waist. "Don't worry. It should work fine, but I need you to strap each person into the harness real tight so that my partner and I can both pull the rope up. Are you familiar with climbing gear?"

Hardy looked at Eric and said, "Well, I used to be in the marines years ago, and we did all kinds of stuff back then. Recently I helped Andy over there climb at the gym, so I know how the newer equipment works." He nodded. "It shouldn't be a problem."

Eric rolled up his shirtsleeve to reveal a tattoo of the Marines Corp logo, an eagle standing on a globe with an anchor set behind it. He said, "Sempre Fi!" and shook Hardy's hand. "We can do this!" Then Eric clipped his harness onto the rope and stepped out of the doorway, disappearing into the falling snow.

Within a flash, Eric returned with one end of the winch cable and attached it to the door handle on the bus. He set up a second harness on the rope that was secured to the cable by a carabiner so that whoever was on the rope would slide easily along the cable to keep them stable as they ascended the planned pathway to the road. Then Hardy asked for a volunteer to be the first scout up the rope. Three boys jumped at the chance, and one, Andy's friend Manny, was soon in the harness. Eric passed Hardy a small handheld walkie-talkie to use for communications and then signaled George to start pulling.

He and Manny vanished up the slope into the snow flurries.

When Eric and Manny were up on the road, Eric sent the harness back down on the rope along the cable, and Hardy secured another scout into it. He called Eric on the radio, and the next boy went up the rope to the road. The system worked smoothly, highlighting Eric's expertise and experience with mountain rescue methods. After ten boys had made it up the slope and had squeezed into the Jeep to warm up, Eric said they needed a break. Their arms were burning from the tugging.

As they waited, Hardy and Blue sat by the door of the bus and looked out as the last flakes of the storm settled down outside. Then Hardy heard a rustling sound far away and stood up to see what was happening. He looked up the slope just as a big slough of snow came down the avalanche chute right at him. He barely had time to duck inside and let the snow flow over the bus, shooting over the doorway like a waterfall and continuing down the slope.

The bus shifted its position slightly in response to the new snow outside. Hardy looked at the scared faces of the four remaining boys and Martha, who was sitting next to the still-unconscious Lori. The plan was to send all able-bodied people up first and then Eric would come down again to take Lori up, with Hardy bringing up the rear. Hardy thought it was taking a long time to get the kids up the slope, so he radioed Eric.

"Hey, Eric. We need to get going again. That snow slide moved the bus a little. If we get another, we may have some trouble down here. What do you hear from the road-clearing guys?"

"Hardy, copy that," Eric said over the radio, his voice distant in the sea of static background noise. "The road crew is making progress, but they've had more snow to . . . usual from a typical storm. The sheriff . . . snowcat out ahead of them, and they found several smaller slides . . . will take some time to clear. They say they'll not be able to get the road clear to us until tomorrow. Then they'll tackle the big avalanche we see here. They're going to have to send choppers to get us out. Let's hope the snow doesn't pick back up. Anyway, we're ready to continue now . . . volunteer scouts are going to help pull the rope, so it should go pretty quickly now. Here comes the harness!"

They got the system going again, one child at a time. Finally, Andy, the last of the boys, went up to safety. When the harness came back down, it was Martha's turn, and she was frantic with fear. Hardy tried to calm her down, but nothing helped. Finally, she held her breath and started up the slope, fretting the whole way.

That left only Hardy, Lori, and Blue. Snow began to slide down the chute in small sloughs. Hardy had a bad feeling as he looked up the long side of the mountain.

Eric arrived as planned with some extra rigging to attach Lori to the rope. Because she was unconscious, Eric would have to bundle her up more securely than the others and carry much of her weight on himself to keep her from dragging on the snow. Hardy and Blue would be the last to leave, like the captains of a sinking ship. Hardy didn't like the analogy.

Blue seemed to pick up on his thoughts and muttered a woof or two.

"OK, Hardy. Here goes."

Eric and Lori set off and were halfway up to the road when another big slough came barreling down the chute, nearly hitting them as it roared by, and plowed into the bus.

Eric threw himself and Lori flat against the slope as the edge of the slide ground over them. Luckily, there was only snow at the edge of the slide and not debris. After it passed, Eric picked Lori up and trudged onward.

Hardy dove inside the bus to avoid being swept down the mountainside. He felt the bus move and the handle that the cable was attached to seemed about ready to tear loose. The bus shifted backward and down about fifteen degrees, the rear of the vehicle sliding lower than the front. Hardy slid to the back of the bus, and Blue fell on top of him. He climbed on his hands and knees up to the door as another smaller slough came down the chute next to them.

Somehow Eric had continued up to the road, and Lori was safe. He radioed to Hardy. "That was really close. Some snow hit Lori, but she's OK, I think." He paused for a moment. "Look!

That last slide pulled the cable so tight that the Jeep . . . right up against the highway guardrail. Any harder and it . . . us over the side of the road or torn the winch off the Jeep. I'm sending the harness back down to you now. You've gotta clip on as fast as you can and then I'll slack off the cable enough for you to unhook it from the bus. That way I can still get you up before . . . weird shit happens to the bus. All right?"

Hardy listened and thought what Eric proposed sounded good, except for one thing. What about Blue? "Say, Eric. I don't understand." He clutched the radio as he spoke. "How are we going to get Blue up there? Do you have an extra harness for him to use? I can bring him up with me then."

"Look, Hardy," Eric said over the radio. "I know you want your dog with you, but there isn't time to get him up here too. We'll just have to leave him there and hope to God we . . . up here before . . . the Jeep over the side. Maybe the dog can climb up here on his own. I don't know. But you have to leave now, man." He pleaded, "*Now!*"

Hardy looked at his best friend and then up the long slope to the highway. There was no way Blue was going to climb up that slope on snow and ice. He felt the bus shift under him and sighed. He hooked up his harness to the cable and the rope. He felt the slack come into the cable as Eric backed off the tension on the winch. He unhooked it from the handle on the bus, and the big vehicle eased away an inch or two when he did that.

It felt like the bus was unstable and was slowly moving ever so slightly, sliding back away from the tree like a dying dinosaur or a ship about to go under. Soon the tree would not support it, and it would fall backward down the slope and over the cliff below.

Hardy took the radio. "I guess I'm ready on this end. Cable unhooked."

He felt the tension on the rope as the people above began to tug at his harness. He looked at Blue, and the dog seemed to know what was about to happen.

"This is it, boy," Hardy said. "Time to go!"

Blue looked at him expectantly with his sad eyes, knowing that whatever happened would be very dangerous, risking a snowy end. Hardy leaned back into the harness, letting it take all his weight, and let go with his hands. Then he opened his arms.

"Come on, Blue! It's goin' to be rough, but we can make it."

With a woof, Blue jumped as high as he could into Hardy's arms. Hardy held the dog tight to his body and they set off, being pulled up the hard snow slope. It was tough for Hardy to keep up with the rate that the rope was moving. He was just barely able to stay on his feet.

***

High up on the avalanche chute, the final section of the snowfield collapsed and began to move with a thunderous roar as thousands of tons of snow and ice commenced a wild trajectory down the mountain, picking up speed as it went. The rumble was deafening and grew louder as it careened down the chute. The sound echoed off the valley walls.

Trees that had held on to the sides of the big field snapped under the strain and were swept away, crushed into tinder in the massive flow. In seconds, the avalanche rushed down to the highway below, riding on the smooth surface of the slide from the night before.

Everyone on the highway heard the roar above them and cringed at the sound. The boys who were helping pull the rope up let go and ran away from the avalanche, afraid for their lives. Eric and George were left to hold Hardy and Blue's weight and were pulled right up to the guardrail, holding on with all their strength to keep Hardy from falling down the slope.

"We can't hold him!" George shouted. "We can't pull him up. We're going to lose Hardy!"

Eric bent low to throw his body against the guardrail as the rope nearly ripped his arms from their sockets.

"Hold on, George!" he shouted. "Hold on to Hardy!"

Then another set of hands gripped the rope behind them, and Martha gritted her teeth as she braced against the Jeep. Then Timmy and Manny grabbed the rope too, fighting to save their loyal bus driver.

***

Hardy and Blue heard the crack of the ice breaking overhead and the following roar of the avalanche speeding down the chute toward them. They were terrified by the deafening sound, and Blue yelped with fear. Hardy felt the rope drop, and he lost his footing. He fell down the slope for a few feet before the rope caught him again. He lost his balance and rolled to the side, holding Blue tightly in his arms. They rolled over each other sideways as they swung like a pendulum to their right, away from the bus and the avalanche and directly below the Jeep above them. But the rope held, and they came to a stop on Hardy's back.

The avalanche was bigger than the one last night. It formed a giant cloud as it hurled along the chute, with rocks and chunks of wood crashing down its core. It ground down the rocks under it. When the leading edge reached the bus, the vehicle simply vanished into the maelstrom and was swept away. The cloud of fine snow and dust swept over Hardy and Blue, and they could see nothing except a white blizzard of snow.

***

"Let me take the weight," George said, "and you go start the winch. Hardy's hooked into the cable and the rope. We can pull him up with the winch!"

Eric ran to the Jeep and started reeling in the cable. It took a while to take up the slack until the locking hook on the end came up to Hardy's level and stuck on the carabiner in his harness. Then the cable took up the weight, and they knew that Hardy began to rise up the slope again.

***

Hardy held on to Blue tightly. "Don't worry, Blue. We'll make it OK. Just you wait and see."

Old Blue was as still as stone in Hardy's arms—covered by a half-inch rime of white powder that encased him from nose to tail. Then he shook his head to rid himself of the coating and woofed. He looked up at Hardy with his sad eyes. He licked Hardy's face to take off some of the snow that had caked over his features during the slide event. Hardy's eyes teared up with joy in spite of the snow.

Up they went, and Hardy managed to turn around so that he could get his feet under him as they rose up the slope.

When Hardy reached the guardrail, Eric stopped the winch and came out to the railing to help pull Hardy and Blue onto the road. They were all safe. Hardy leaned on the fender of the Jeep.

He wouldn't let Blue go. The scouts all gathered around him in awe, patting Blue and asking questions a mile a minute. Hardy couldn't talk at first.

Eric said, "Well, I'll be damned. You held the dog all this way?" He reached out and petted Blue on the head and grinned. "Hardy, you're one tough son of a gun! He must mean a lot to you."

"Eric, I can't tell you how much that dog means to me. I could never leave him." Then he tried again to explain. "You know, we marines never leave a man behind." He tried to chuckle.

"Hardy, I should have known better than to even suggest such a thing." Eric used his glove to swipe some of the snow off Blue's back. "His name is Blue, right?"

"You're looking at the royal personage called Blue." Hardy turned away to hide his emotions. "He's my best friend."

"Well, I'm pleased to formally meet you, Blue."

They stood there a couple of minutes while a few of the kids and Martha retreated to the warm interior of the Jeep.

"Let's get you two inside the car to warm up. I'll see if Mrs. Reynolds is through crying yet."

"Crying? Why's that woman crying? Is she all right?"

"It seems her husband has been desperately trying to get ahold of her. They talked on the radio, and she's been crying ever since." He shook his head and chuckled.

"And we have a Flight for Life helicopter landing in a few minutes to check everybody out." Eric looked in the rear window of the Jeep. "They'll take Lori Phillips to the hospital in Durango. I think she'll be OK. They'll take her son, too, so that they can be together. We hope to have other choppers here to get the rest of you down from the mountain soon."

Hardy couldn't believe that fortune had changed so quickly for him and his passengers. He got into the back seat of the Jeep while Martha was still sobbing in the front seat. He was afraid to ask her what was so upsetting that she was suffering a torrent of tears. He chanced it, having survived an avalanche with her. But her answer made no sense to him.

She said, "Roger told me he loved me! And we don't have to move to Denver if I don't want to. Isn't that nice? What a wonderful man."

Hardy sat there with Old Blue by his side and thought, Yeah. That's what life is all about. Isn't it, old boy?

As the helicopter came in for a landing, Old Blue gave Hardy his sad-eyed look and wagged his tail in agreement.

Black Storm on White Mountain

Hardy Harris, retired Marine Corps sergeant, sat in the cab of his Ford F-150 pickup truck with his constant canine companion, Old Blue. They were watching a herd of twenty-four wild horses grazing on the hillside nearby. The herd was spread out over a wide area on the peaceful landscape that lay on the west ridge of White Mountain. From his vantage point on the ridge, he had a comfortable view of the mustangs and a complete overview of the city of Green River and the confluence of Green River with Bitter Creek below. The valley was bracketed by Wilkins Peak to the south and White Mountain to the north.

White Mountain was a mesa, a huge table-like structure, measuring up to forty miles long from north to south and about twenty-five miles wide. It rose about fourteen hundred feet above the valley that bounded it on all sides. At its southern edge, an ancient lava flow capped a portion of the bedrock, forming an even higher point called Pilot Butte that rose an additional four hundred feet above the rolling surface of the rest of the mountain.

Old Blue was Hardy's aging basset hound, who had brown and black patches on an otherwise white to gray coat. He lay on the truck seat at Hardy's side. Blue derived his name from an area of bluish fur on his shoulders where patches of three different colors converged to yield a grayish-blue tint. It was a spot that was petted by all the children on the school bus that Hardy drove as his main occupation and where Blue rode shotgun during the school year.

"Let's move around this little hill and see if we can get a better view of that big black stallion, shall we?" Hardy started the truck and rolled slowly forward along the rough gravel road, around the slope of the small hillock that separated them from the herd. When he found a good vantage point, he stopped the truck and turned off the engine. He and Blue resumed their enjoyable pastime of watching the horses, with Hardy snapping a few photographs of the magnificent creatures.

After a minute or two, Hardy said, "Hey, where did that big black stallion go to? He was here just before we moved." Hardy scanned the hillside for the majestic leader of the herd, a great muscular horse with a jet-black coat and no markings on him at all. The horse had a full mane and a tail that he held high as he loped around the herd, keeping individual mares from spreading out too far from the rest of the group. He was always on the lookout for any sort of trouble that might threaten his family.

Hardy searched all around for the black stallion but did not see him with the other horses. Then Blue uttered a quiet woof and turned to look out the window on the opposite side of the truck. Hardy followed Blue's gaze and said, "Well, I'll be damned."

He looked out the window at the big black leader who had walked around the hillock and was now staring at Hardy, Blue, and the pickup. He was on full alert as he watched them, with his ears pricked forward and his long black tail swishing back and forth. He seemed as curious about them as they were about his herd. He had come around the hill to check them out and to ensure that his mares were safe. The horse whinnied at them and then turned in a rush, galloping away over the top of the hill and rejoining his herd.

"Well, that was something," Hardy said as he reached over to pat Blue on the shoulders. "He sneaked up on us to see what we were doing, Blue." He looked Blue in the eye and asked, "What kind of a guard dog are you, anyway?"

***

Later that evening, Hardy sipped a cool can of Coors Banquet beer while stretched out on his folding camp chair. He had chosen a campsite on the slope just below Pilot Butte because of the view. When the sun went down in the west, he would have a ringside seat for the glorious event.

He reached over and patted Blue on the ribs, and the old dog managed to twitch an ear in appreciation.

Hardy enjoyed the breeze that rose from the west and carried the scent of dry grass and sagebrush to his attention. He really liked this country and its wide-open spaces, something he had learned to love growing up on a farm in South Dakota. His career had carried him away to some of the far corners of the world, Vietnam as a marine, California for business, and finally back to the South Dakota where he married and settled down in Pierre, selling insurance with his dear wife, Lily. After a few years they moved to Durango, Colorado, where Lily taught school. They had had a fine life until cancer took her from him a few years ago. Living in the mountains of Colorado, his thoughts never left Lily for very long.

Blue raised his head, listened to a rustle in the grass nearby, and issued a low woof to show he was on guard. Well, as much on guard as he could be lying on his side, apparently daydreaming about potential ground squirrels in the area.

Hardy stood up and stretched a moment on his way to the cooler for a second Coors. The sun was arcing down on the horizon, where only a few scattered clouds were highlighted by a fantastic orange glow as rays of red shot out in a starburst from the setting sun. He raised his hand and blocked the harshest rays, squinting at the sunset, his tanned and wrinkled face forming a smile at the sight.

"Well, Blue, that's one heck of a sunset." He looked at Blue, who responded by rolling into an upright position and woofing agreement.

"I sure wish Lori and Andy could be here too." Blue wagged his tail and looked toward the setting sun.

Lori and Andy Phillips had planned this camping trip with Hardy all summer to coincide with antelope hunting season, which opened in this area in late September. Then Andy came down with the flu, and Lori had to cancel until the boy recovered. Hardy had soldiered on with the understanding that they would join him in Rock Springs as soon as Andy could travel. So he had set out with food for three, a couple of cases of beer, and a supply of Blue's favorite dog chow and treats.

He hoped the boy would get well soon. Their lives were heavily intertwined since they had survived an ordeal one winter in the Colorado mountains. Now he viewed Lori as an adopted daughter and Andy as the grandson he had never had. They had shared all sorts of activities together like Cub Scouts, hunting, fishing, and camping. Lori had welcomed Hardy into their family to fill the void left when her husband had died in a truck wreck. They were now his family in Durango.

"Come on, Blue," he said softly as dusk settled and the sunset began to really show its glory. "Let's get a better view." He walked out along a small ridge from their campsite. Blue followed carefully in his master's tracks and avoided any sharp objects that might project through the base of the sage.

They stopped on a flattened area where humans or animals had stood before, probably due to the view that position gave of the slopes below. Hardy clicked away with his small pocket Canon digital camera. He still preferred older technology rather than his cell phone to take pictures. He'd send a photo to Lori later with a text: "Wish you were here."

Just as the last light bled out of the sky, Blue jumped up and began barking. A sudden thunder broke the silence as a stampede of wild horses appeared below the ridge. Twenty to thirty wild mustangs galloped across the sage-filled landscape, running at full speed in a panic. Hardy could see the wild look of their eyes—they were that close—and could tell from their neighing that they were being chased by something terrifying.

A white mare led the herd in flight, with a multicolored horde of white, black, sorrel, and paint horses, young and old, all following at her heels. Young foals ran beside their mothers, eyes wild, as the mares tried to protect their young. The black stallion, big and muscular, brought up the rear, keeping stragglers in motion and stopping occasionally to rear up and paw at some unseen foe that cursed them in their flight. He screamed at the invisible menace and galloped onward to defend his herd.

The sky grew darker, and Blue barked at the black sky in front of them as a buzzing sound filled the air.

"What the hell?" Hardy swore as he saw some little blue lights flicker through the sky like a small swarm of neon-blue fireflies. They disappeared into the night in the direction taken by the wild horses. The buzzing sound followed them.

Blue barked. *Baroo! Baroo!* He ran a short way down the ridge in chase but stopped as the lights flew away.

"Jeez, Blue. What the devil was that?" Hardy turned to where the lights had faded into the distance. Blue stopped barking and ran over to Hardy, growling and bounding on his short legs, more excited than Hardy had seen him in months.

They could still hear the horses pounding along to their left, but darkness now obscured the view. In two minutes, even the sound of the hoofbeats had vanished.

***

After breakfast the next morning, Hardy loaded up man's best friend in his pickup and drove south along the rutted dirt track that descends from Pilot Butte. When they reached the portion of the hill where the angle eased off, they found a thirty-foot-wide trail of trampled grass and sagebrush created by the stampeding horses the night before. It crossed at right angles to the dirt road they were on, heading northeast around the base of the butte.

"Those horses must have been scared to death," Hardy said as he stepped out of the truck and viewed the damage. Blue stayed in the pickup but stood on the front seat and then put his paws up on the windowsill for a better view. He woofed. He had seen or heard something in the direction the horses had run.

"You hear something?" Hardy got in the truck and turned it off the dirt road to follow the mustangs' trail. "Let's go see if we can find those ponies, shall we?"

He shifted into four-wheel drive and crept along the trampled trail. The horses were easy enough to track. The path they had taken varied in width but was clearly discernable in the morning light. The truck easily pushed through the vegetation, finding traction in the pale, sunbaked soil. Grasses of varying types covered the ground and made up the bulk of the feed the horses lived on. Here and there the soil was sandy or had become tan powder from the summer heat. They encountered a few gullies that crossed the path, coming down from the upper slope of Pilot Butte and running straight downhill to their right. The gullies ran out on the flatter ground at the base of the slope.

The mustangs had taken a course that arced northwest around the base of the butte and then turned north along the broad ridge of White Mountain. Hardy wondered what could have caused them to run so far.

Within half a mile, Hardy saw movement and heard a horse neighing. He crept the truck forward until he spotted a dusky-colored mare limping along ahead of them, its eyes filled with pain and fear as it looked back at the truck. Mustangs don't generally trust motor vehicles—or helicopters or humans, for that matter. These machines were often used to chase them when people wanted to do them harm.

Hardy hit the brakes hard, and the truck came to an abrupt halt just as the front left wheel reached the edge of a three-foot-deep wash that crossed the track. Blue slid forward on the front seat, but his claws dug into the cloth, saving him from the indignity of a crash onto the floor.

"You OK, boy?" Hardy shut the vehicle down, opened his door, stepped out, and then waited to lift Blue to the ground. They walked over and inspected the wash. They found an easy spot where both of their sets of legs could descend and crossed over to the other side. They approached the horse, who eyed them both suspiciously, especially the short, spotted wolf by Hardy's side.

The horse hobbled away a few steps, puffing heavily through her nostrils, nickering softly as she moved. Hardy could see that her left front leg was badly broken. Bone punched through the skin and dangled loosely. The horse's other front leg was oddly shaped and swollen, but she somehow managed to stand on it. After a few hops, she stumbled and gazed ahead in the direction the herd and gone. She thrust her head that way and whinnied.

"Damn it, Blue," Hardy said gravely. "She's in bad shape. She broke her leg running through this rough ground in the dark. She's done for with that injury."

He thought about the rifle that hung on the rack in the back window of the pickup. The .308-caliber Ruger American rifle would put the suffering animal out of her misery. But he was not authorized to kill a wild mustang, no matter how humane such an act would be. He would go into town and report what he had seen to the proper authorities. Then they could come out and do the deed. That would make it legal, even if the animal suffered a little longer.

Hardy called out to the horse that they would be back, as if she could understand him. He and Blue climbed into the pickup and turned it around. In thirty minutes, they were back to the rutted dirt track headed for Rock Springs on a convoluted road network that crossed the east flank of White Mountain.

***

An hour later, Hardy and Blue entered the office of the Federal Bureau of Land Management that was located two miles northeast of Rock Springs off Highway 191. This was the location of the field office that managed the wild horse population for the southwestern part of Wyoming. *"Management" might not be the most appropriate word for the job the BLM did with the wild horses*, Hardy thought. He knew that the agency largely ignored the horses until important landowners complained they ate too much grass on the wild lands the ranchers leased for feeding their own cattle. Then to appease the ranchers and at the same time thin the mustang herds, the agency would round up a bunch of horses selected randomly but casually, reducing their numbers. The roundups killed a few animals by chasing them all over the high prairie with helicopters and other vehicles.

"Jeez, Blue," he said. "I hope that wasn't some new kind of BLM roundup we saw last night. It seemed cruel."

Hardy stepped up to the long Formica-covered counter that blocked the public from BLM personnel. He called out to an empty room.

As he waited for a response, he caught a glimpse of his profile in a mirror that hung on the wall near the end of the counter right next to a bulletin board full of notices and memos. He realized that he looked more rustic than usual given the few days' growth of stubble on his face and quickly combed brown locks that peeked out from under the Stetson he wore. His friendly brown eyes peered out of a lean, tanned face that betrayed his time spent out of doors. It wasn't the prettiest face, but he was used to its rugged character and broad smile.

After three minutes, a portly woman dressed in a beige agency shirt and olive-colored pants walked into the room through a back door. She was finishing a sandwich and seemed unaware that Hardy was at the counter until he said, "Howdy. My name's Hardy Harris."

"Oh," she said, surprised. "Didn't hear the bell when you came in the door."

Hardy turned around and looked for a bell by the entrance. Seeing none, he said, "Say, I wanted to report a seriously injured wild horse that I saw up on White Mountain this morning."

"An injured mustang?" The woman came up to her side of the counter and seemed officious. "Well, thank you for telling us about the horse. I'll make a note for our wildlife manager to look into it just as soon as he gets back into town."

"When will that be, ma'am?"

She looked at a calendar that lay flat on the counter. "Let's see . . . that will most likely be Monday." She looked up at Hardy and smiled. "Maybe sooner if he comes back early."

"But today is Monday. You mean today?" Hardy fixed his eyes on the woman as he clarified. "Or do you mean *next* Monday—a week from now?"

"Next Monday," she said. "You see, most of the office personnel are in Denver for a week of meetings and training classes—you know, classes for sexual harassment and bullying—that kind of stuff."

"This horse ain't going to make it till next Monday, ma'am. Its leg is broken." Hardy thought the woman didn't understand him. "Its leg is broken in a compound fracture. It'll never heal itself. Someone must put it down."

The woman suddenly reacted as if Hardy was a madman. "Now you wait right there, mister." She put on a stern face and stood up to her full bureaucratic height. "Nobody can make a decision like that except a trained wildlife health manager."

Hardy didn't understand what had set her off except that he might have stepped on someone's bureaucratic toes. He'd dealt with petty clerks before. "I'm not saying I'm going to shoot anything, ma'am. But someone should take a look at this poor animal and put it out of its misery."

The woman gave Hardy a once-over and picked up a handheld radio. She held him in a contemptuous stare and pushed the talk button.

"HQ to Wild Bill. HQ to Wild Bill." She looked expectant. "Wild Bill, you there?"

There was a pause that became a long wait as the woman made the call again. Hardy wondered if Wild Bill was a lawman of some sort and if he was in trouble somehow.

"Harriet, I told you not to call me that over the radio." A stern and clearly frustrated man's voice crackled back over the airwaves. "What's troubling you now? You getting bored back in the office?"

The woman—Harriet—turned away from Hardy and walked from the counter toward the far end of the room, where she carried on a heated but quiet conversation with Wild Bill. After a few minutes, she returned to the counter, her face a mask of placidity.

"You need to see William. He's at the corral up Lion Kol Road about two miles from here. Take 191 south to the next turn east and follow that dirt road about a mile. You can't miss it." Then she dismissed Hardy, marching away and disappearing through a door at the back of the room.

***

Hardy pulled into the parking lot next to a small barn just past a low rock outcrop. He stepped out of the truck and tossed Blue a strip of artificial bacon to keep him occupied while he stayed behind in the vehicle.

Hardy heard the sound of horses neighing and a man calling out from the back of the barn, so he walked toward the commotion. Behind the barn, a six-foot-high line of two-inch by two-inch mesh cyclone fence closed off the end of a shallow canyon where horses were being kept. Hardy climbed up the slope overlooking the canyon that contained at least two acres of corral and holding pens as well as a covered feeding station for the animals. A lean-to ran along the face of the cliff on one side of the facility, providing shelter from the elements for the mustangs.

A man on horseback, wearing a ten-gallon hat, chaps, and a deep-blue shirt under a tan jacket, was riding a tall brown-and-white spotted horse. The man and horse were working a half dozen mustangs to cut them from another fifteen or so horses and drive them into one of the two corrals. The mustangs didn't want to be separated from their amigos, so they tried any number of tricks for getting back together. The man held up a coiled lariat in his left hand and kept his horse's reins in his right. He made small movements with his body and legs to control the painted cutting horse as it dodged left and right, managing the mustangs. Finally, the six horses entered the corral, and a young boy swung the corral gate shut to contain the troublesome six. The man then wheeled his horse around and dispersed the remaining mustangs.

Only then did the man notice Hardy, raising his left hand to the brim of his hat in acknowledgment. He rode his horse next to the fence by the barn and dismounted. The boy took the horse and rope from him, and the man came through the gate and shook hands with Hardy.

"Name's William Hickok, Mr. Harris. You can call me Bill." Hickok took his gloves off and waved toward the doorway into the barn. "Follow me while I get some of this gear off."

Hickok led Hardy to the tack room inside and proceeded to take off his leather chaps, spurs, and jacket. He hung the chaps on a nail on the side of the room. "Sometimes those boys try biting your leg, so I leather up for tight quarters."

He looked Hardy over carefully, starting with his Stetson and leather vest, down to the worn but clean blue Levi's and scuffed black ropers, Hardy's favorite driving boots.

"You ride much, Mr. Harris?"

"Used to when I was growing up back in South Dakota. We used horses to ride the fence line and chase cows."

"Good to know." Hickok led Hardy over to a small makeshift office in one corner of the tack room. "Here—set down and tell me what brought you out this way."

Hardy sat down and told Hickok what he had seen during the night and that morning. While he did so, he watched Hickok for his reactions and sized the man up for himself.

William "Bill" Hickok, called Wild Bill in his younger days, was now a stocky, sixtysomething gentleman, a couple of inches shorter than Hardy's six one frame. He had long sandy-colored hair that came down to his shirt collar, sideburns, a flamboyant mustache that he combed out to the sides, and a goatee. He had pale-blue eyes in a weather-beaten face with nice features overall. With the ten-gallon hat on, he looked like a reincarnation of his namesake—at least as far as Hardy could tell from photographs he had seen of the famous gunslinger. Hickok had an expressive face that changed with the conversation and his mood. He frowned once he took in all of Hardy's story.

"So we got an injured horse wandering around up on White Mountain, and I need to get up there and probably put it down. That about right, Hardy?"

"Yes, sir. I think so."

"OK then." Hickok sprang up and walked over to a vertical cabinet where he extracted a Winchester .30-06 bolt-action rifle with telescopic sights mounted on it. He fished out a box of shells for the weapon and started for the door.

"I'll drive and you can show me where that mare is. OK?"

"That sounds fine, but I'll need to bring my dog with us. Can't leave him alone too long." Hardy stopped and waited for Hickok's response. "Any problem?"

"No, no. That's fine." Hickok walked to a tan-colored official BLM Dodge Ram pickup and started making room in the front seat for his fellow occupants. He hung the rifle on the rack in the back window of the cab.

By that time, Hardy showed up and lifted Blue into the front seat floor of the Ram. Hickok climbed inside, buckled up, and said, "What kind of a dog is that? He's all ears and body. He ain't got no legs hardly at all." He chuckled as Blue took in his words.

Hardy smiled, used to being chastised for his choice of K9 companion. "Well, Blue and I go back a long way. He's my best friend, and we keep each other's secrets."

Hickok backed the truck up and then swung it around and down the gravel road smoothly. As he drove out to the highway, he reached over and scratched one of Blue's ears.

"Well, good thing I like dogs." He patted Blue's head. "Say, he's not one of those ones that barks funny, is he? You know— wooo, wooo, wooo?"

Hardy laughed. "Don't worry. You'll know when you hear him."

***

It took an hour to drive back up to White Mountain where Hardy and Blue had seen the injured mare. She had managed to limp her way another hundred yards along the path that her herd had traveled. As they drove up, she lost her footing and went down on her front knees from exhaustion. She stayed like that— half up and half down—and turned her head to see what the truck was up to. In doing so, she lost her balance and rolled onto her side. She flailed for about thirty seconds, legs clawing the air as she rolled back and forth, trying to get her feet under her. Then she lay still on her right side with her head on the ground, breathing hard.

"Well, she's a goner with that leg broke like that." Hickok got out of the truck and lifted his rifle from the gun rack. He pulled four cartridges from the ammo box on the seat, loaded one in the rifle's chamber, and pocketed the other three. "You better keep Blue in here till I'm done. I don't want to scare the poor thing any more than I have to."

He closed the truck door and walked in a big arc around the injured horse. She tracked him from her grounded position, watching him circle around to face her head-on, with the truck well off to his right. Then he talked to her in gentle words while he lined up a shot. The horse seemed to know what was happening and protested weakly.

There was a sharp crack, and the horse's head fell to the ground. Hickok came closer and shot twice more, ensuring the beast was dead. Then he walked up and inspected the mare. Hardy joined him by the horse's side.

"Damn fine animal," Hardy said. "Shame she had to go like this."

"Yeah, it is." Hickok spit some tobacco juice on the ground. "But she didn't have a chance with a broken leg. These animals live on their feet, and out here it's the law of the range. You got to move constantly to find grass and water. These horses cover up to twenty miles every day."

Hardy examined the horse's broken leg. "Good God—this bone is completely shattered. No way it would heal back."

"Even an expensive racehorse would be put down with a leg like that," Hickok whispered. "It still don't make me feel any better about killing the poor creature."

They walked back to the truck, and Hickok radioed his office. He asked Harriet to contact a local rancher who recovered dead animals and have him call Hickok for exact directions to the carcass. Then he walked out and attached a tag to the horse's leg and tied orange-colored surveyors ribbon to the tallest sagebrush on either side of the animal.

"Winston should be able to see that when he comes lookin'." He cast his eyes north along the path the herd had run during the night. "We better follow this path a ways and see what other destruction is waiting out there."

Hardy, Blue, and Hickok returned to the truck, and Hickok motored for another mile along the trampled path made by the mustangs on the rolling shoulder of the mesa. The ground was rough, and Hickok had to angle down the sides of some gullies and washes as they traveled. He came to a rise where he stopped the truck, got out, and scanned the landscape ahead of them. He passed his binoculars to Hardy.

"They ran out along the ridge there for another couple of miles. Then I lose track. The mountain forms a long broad ridge for a few miles beyond that falls away on either side in a series of valleys, some to the right, some left."

Hardy followed the track with his eyes as Hickok spoke. He couldn't see how much farther the ridge extended. "How far does the ridge go, Bill?"

"It has its ups and downs, but a ridge of some sort continues along the east rim another twenty miles toward the north edge of the mesa. That's where the Green River cuts back west from the Wind River Range. You can see the Wind River Mountains up there in the distance."

Hardy scanned farther north and saw the snowy peaks just at the edge of his vision. Haze rose as the day warmed up and obscured details of the wild, open spaces ahead.

"You said you saw a black stallion running along with this herd, right? Big herd of at least twenty horses?"

"Yeah, that's right. Big, beautiful animal. Jet black, as I recall."

"That must be Stormy, all right, with his herd. They call him Black Storm 'cause he's a devil of a fighter when it comes to defending his herd. No other stallion can successfully steal mares from his harem." Bill smiled as he spoke. He pointed to Pilot Butte, which rose above them to their west. "He usually has his herd out on the west ridge this time of year. That's where the best grass is now."

Hardy handed the binos back to Hickok. "What do we do now? Keep following?"

"No. This country gets rough up ahead, so the truck is not very good goin'. We'd need horses to cover that area." He paused and looked at Hardy. "I'd like to see what's scaring these critters. Something tells me it might happen again tonight." He took his hat off and ran his fingers over his head, smoothing out his long hair. Then he put his hat on and looked to the west at the sun and then at Pilot Butte. He began climbing into the Ram.

Hardy and Blue loaded up too.

"If you don't mind some company for the night, I might bring my rig up here and camp next to you. Seems to me you have the best overlook of this part of the mountain. Maybe we can see what's goin' on up here."

"Sure. Sounds all right to me."

They headed down the slope eastward a half mile. There they encountered a two-track dirt trail that Hickok drove to the main dirt road that followed the southern rim of the mountain.

They agreed that Hickok would drop Hardy back at his truck and then make arrangements for the next day. He would return before dark to Hardy's campsite, driving his own personal pickup with a camper shell on the back. They would meet up then.

***

"Sure is beautiful country up here," Hardy commented later that evening, taking a sip of Coors. He and Bill were sitting on camp chairs on the shoulder of Pilot Butte. From their location, they had a sprawling view of the south and southwest side of White Mountain's grassier slopes. They could see several small herds of wild horses scattered below them and to the west, grazing as the evening came on.

They experienced a wonderful sunset but also observed the first high clouds that signaled a change in the weather from the northwest. The smell of moisture was in the air.

"Storms usually blow up big on White Mountain because of the terrain," Hickok said. "The wind can be vicious, and this time of year, there can be rain or sleet, even snow if the temperature dips low enough." He paused and scanned the oncoming clouds. "The wild horses look for a bit of shelter from the wind and have to tough it out."

The sunset was impressive, lighting up the high clouds with orange flames, red fire rimming the mountaintops. Hardy took a photo with his cell phone this time so that he could send it directly to Lori and Andy. Bill took a snapshot, even though he must have seen that sunset a hundred times before.

Then Blue stood up and woofed.

The sun had set and darkness was easing their view of the mountains into the night, but they heard whinnying come to their ears from the west. Blue stared westward and went on point as much as he could, directing their attention toward one band of horses about two miles away and below them.

Hardy and Bill stood up and raised their binoculars, viewing the herd. They saw the horses begin to bunch up and gallop as a group to the east. A stallion reared up as if to ward off an unseen menace and then dropped to all fours to run with his family. There were lots of snorts and screams of fear from the animals as they ran in the semidarkness. The sounds came to the men seconds after the horses began moving.

"You see anything chasing them?" Bill asked Hardy.

"Not a thing. But they're still far away."

The horses came in a rush to the east, getting closer to Pilot Butte as they arced around its steeper slopes. In a few minutes, they were less than a mile away, following a course similar to the one taken by the horses the night before. This was a smaller herd of maybe sixteen animals. The thunder of their hooves on the earth reached the men as they approached.

"There," Hardy said, looking through his binoculars. "The blue lights."

"Got 'em." Bill dropped his binos and picked up a set of night vision glasses he had brought with him. "There—I can see the lights in the air. They're kind of a neon blue, about eight of them, all spread out."

"Yeah, I see them too." Hardy lowered his binos as Blue began to woof threateningly. "Listen. You can hear that buzzing sound now."

They both listened and watched as the horses gradually turned to the northeast around the butte to head north. "Well, I'll be damned," Bill said. "I can see them now—not just the lights but also what the lights are riding on."

"What is it?"

"Drones!" Bill shouted. "Someone is chasing horses with drone helicopters."

"At night? That's crazy. Let me see."

"And a bunch of drones acting like a herding crew." Hickok lowered his night vision glasses and handed them to Hardy.

They stood in the light of a single Coleman lantern that lit the camp. "How the devil are they doing that?"

"Damn good question. Don't you need one man to pilot each one of those quadcopter jobs?"

"That's what I thought, but maybe they can be programmed and act as a cluster for certain uses." Bill took the glasses back. "Well, they're heading north along the ridge."

"Should we chase them?"

"No point in the dark. They can move a lot faster than us on wheels." Bill hesitated. "But I think I know where they're going.

There are only three or four places where you can get in to corral and load horses up that way."

"So you think that someone is stealing these horses?"

"Hardy, I know someone is rustling those animals. No one would go to this much trouble to drive them up that ridge unless they had a plan. It's just a new way of doin' it."

"What can we do?"

Bill pulled out his cell phone. "I gotta make a few calls a fore tomorrow." He started dialing. "You doin' anything special tomorrow?" He looked at Hardy.

"Nothing that can't be changed."

"How about riding along with me to see where these mustangs went? You can bring that Ruger bolt-action job I saw in your truck."

"You got yourself a deal, Bill."

***

At 8:00 a.m. the next morning, Hardy and Bill Hickok met John Brannan on the dirt track that ran out the north ridge of White Mountain. John was a part-time wrangler who tended wild horses at the BLM holding facility where Hardy had first met Hickok. He had driven a truck and trailer up the mountain with two saddled horses for Hickok and Hardy to ride as they followed the path taken by the stampeding herd.

They cinched up their saddles, packed saddlebags, and loaded other gear for the day. Hickok had his Winchester with him in a scabbard on his saddle, and Hardy had his Ruger packed similarly. Hickok also had a Colt revolver in a holster on his belt that was strapped down to his right leg. In addition, Hickok had a Mossberg 12-gauge shotgun tied to the back of his saddle. They carried extra ammunition, rain slickers, and packed lunches that John had prepared for them, along with two liters of water each. Hickok had his cell phone and a handheld radio. They were ready for anything.

"Now, John, you stay on your radio. I don't know when or where we're goin' to come off the mountain," Hickok said as he mounted up. "I'll radio you or call you as we proceed. I might lose cell coverage up there, so just stand by. OK?"

"Sure, Bill. Just give me an update when you can."

"Thanks for takin' care of my dog, John." Hardy had arranged to keep Blue occupied while he was away.

"No sweat, Hardy. Blue will be just fine."

With that and a check to be sure Hardy was ready, Hickok reined his horse around and headed north at a trot. Hardy followed suit. They hoped they would be back by nightfall.

Blue barked as he saw them ride off through the brush and tall grass. Hardy heard him but had to press on.

The two men rode a half mile to reach the trampled path created by the wild herd passing in the night. The terrain was rough, with several small gullies cutting across their path. It had rained lightly the night before, enough to moisten the gullies and soften the earth. Otherwise, the ground had largely dried out again.

The sky to the west was well clouded already. It looked like rain would catch up to them by midday. The forecast was for a solid cold front and thunderstorms by late afternoon. After that, all hell could break loose, making their progress a lot more difficult.

After a couple of hours of riding and a few miles of travel, they came to a place along the ridge where two trampled trails converged and formed one swath of flattened vegetation. The grass was shorter in that area, and the brush was only a foot tall. The ground wasn't as uneven as elsewhere.

Hickok pulled up and examined the hoofprints in the dirt. He pointed ahead of them. "This is what I was hoping for. Whoever was driving the herds brought them on a single path. That means they know where they want to take them. But they're avoiding the parts of the ridge that people often use, so no one sees them."

"It really looks like rustling, doesn't it?"

"Yeah, sure enough." Hickok pulled out his water bottle to drink and looked west at the darkening sky. "We're gonna get wet here in a little while, and I don't want to be on the crest of the ridge if we get some lightning. Let's make tracks while we can."

He kicked his horse into a gentle gallop that the animal could maintain for a long period. Hardy did the same, happy to get out of the trotting gait they had used so far. A gallop was a lot smoother ride for him, not being accustomed to the saddle as much as Hickok was.

Hardy watched Hickok ride, impressed by what he saw. Hickok was an adept horseman, one who was obviously comfortable on a working horse. He watched the ground ahead of him, carefully following the tracks of the herd. The horses enjoyed the freedom of the wide-open space as much as the men did.

They covered about three more miles, dropping off the ridge and riding cross-country through the upper portions of valleys where the mountainside slowed them to a trot again. Wind came upon them from the west as the first rain began pelting them. They stopped to pull on rain slickers. At the head of one deep valley that fell away to their left, Hickok radioed John and gave him their location. He didn't consult a map.

"Looks like you know your way around this country," Hardy commented.

Hickok glanced at Hardy as he tucked the radio back on his belt. "Hardy, I been riding these mountains in one way or another for close to fifty years. I've been up and down most of these side valleys on horseback, in a jeep, or on foot, chasing cattle or horses or hunting all my life." He waved his hand in a broad sweep over the whole landscape as he spoke.

"This is God's country, and those wild horses are God's creatures," Hickok said. "They were born to run free up here. I ain't about to let no man interfere with that." He grinned at Hardy. "Come on. We gotta get over this bit of ridge before the heavy downpour catches us out in the open."

As if to emphasize his point, a gust of wind roared at them from the west. Hickok urged his horse forward as the rain picked up, and Hardy followed close behind, driving his horse right on Hickok's tracks.

Tall black clouds suddenly jumped up from the valley to their left. Dark, menacing turbulence churned the clouds higher as they rose up the slope of the mountain. The clouds were rolling now, appearing in two churning stacks that each seemed alive with currents. Lightning began shooting back and forth in the turbulence, going mostly sideways between clouds as the men spurred their horses into a run over the crest of the ridge. To the west, thick stalks of white lightning crashed into the side of the mountain a mile or so behind them.

The sky became so dark above them that it seemed like nightfall as they dropped over the far side of the ridge. The black clouds swept right over them as Hickok raced ahead and down a small valley to the right. Lightning struck the crest where they had just been. Torrential rain engulfed them just as they came to a low copse of trees in the center of the little valley. Hickok reined his horse into a walk and turned him right and then down into a deep gully below the trees. He looked back to be sure Hardy was following. He smiled when he saw Hardy right on his tail.

He stopped his horse in the gully, and Hardy pulled up beside him. The horses were breathing heavily, ears forward and snorting. Their eyes were crazy with excitement as the black storm raged right over their heads. Rain came down in sheets.

Water poured off Hardy's Stetson and ran off the hat's rim in a thin sheet. Lightning cracked all around them, scaring the horses and Hardy half to death. Everything went black except for the flashes of lightning. Hardy felt his horse's panic beneath him and patted him while he spoke soothingly to him. The last thing he wanted was for his horse to bolt out of the gully and into the storm. The horse responded to his confident manner and reassuring words. He saw that Hickok was doing the same with his mount.

The darkness, with flashes of white shafts of light and the roar of thunder, lasted for about ten minutes, then the lightning eased up as it moved over the mountain and down the slope. The sky brightened and the rain let up a little. The two men and their mounts stayed put as water began flowing down the gully they were in.

Hickok walked his horse forward out of the water and a few feet up the slope. He signaled Hardy to do the same. Hardy rode up next to Hickok. "That was a hell of a storm."

"No shit. That was worse than the last time I was here." Hickok started chuckling. Hardy grinned and then joined in the laughter. Hickok dug in his coat pocket as the rain slowed down. He pulled out a small metal flask, opened it, and took a swig. Then he offered the flask to Hardy.

"Brandy."

Hardy took the flask, had a long drink, coughed, and handed it back. "Strong stuff."

"I found this place about twenty years ago when I got caught up here in a storm. I figured if none of these trees showed lightning strikes, it must be safe." He moved his horse a few feet higher on the side of the gully. "We're gonna get a shitload of water down this shoot before long. But the worst of the storm will be over by then. We gotta sit tight awhile longer."

"Is that why you stayed on your horse and didn't dismount?"

"That and the horse is more confident with me on him. He might feel like something was wrong if he felt me abandon ship." Hickok took another swig of brandy. "Besides, if he bolts, I want to go with him and not walk back to town on foot . . . could be embarrassing."

They both laughed.

***

The rain and lightning had Hardy and Hickok pinned down in the gully for nearly two hours before the storm receded. They rode out of the valley and got back on the trail by four o'clock, but they rode slowly in order to follow the path the mustangs had taken. Hickok was one hell of a tracker, but after the heavy rain, a lot of the hoofprints had washed out, and he had to go by the flattened vegetation alone.

Darkness fell early as black, sinuous clouds hung over their heads like a wet blanket of death, just waiting to cut loose in another downpour. Finally, as they crept along, a few breaks appeared in the clouds, and they caught the last rays of sun as night settled over them. Still they rode on, occasional moonlight giving them some sense of the landscape.

They heard a low, ominous sound—one they felt more than heard at first—and recognized it as stampeding hooves. Hickok pointed to the right of the crest of the ridge they were on, reining his horse and moving that way. When he and Hardy were out of the expected path of the onrushing animals, he turned around and untied his shotgun from the back of his saddlebags, pulling it free. He raised it to his shoulder just as the first of a herd of terrified horses appeared, running along the ridge fifty feet away. The horses were wild with fear, snorting and running in the moonlight.

And right behind them about thirty feet in the air came the whirring blue lights, forming a semicircle around the tail end of the herd. The drones dipped and weaved but largely maintained spacing in the arc of neon.

Hickok racked a shell into the shotgun's chamber, pointed the barrel up like he was shooting clay pigeons, and began firing at the lights. He missed at first but then got the right lead on them and fired again and again. Two of the lights fell from the sky, crashing in the dark grass.

The horses ran on into the night for a few hundred yards and then, as a group, turned off the crest. Down into a valley they went, slowing to deal with the slope in the dark. The blue lights dropped back and reformed the arc with fewer drones than before. They continued to drive the horses downward into the valley.

"Let them go, Hardy," Hickok said. "I know where they're headed now." He stopped his horse and pulled out his radio. "Say, Hardy, see if you can find those damn drones that we hit. I gotta make some calls."

Hardy watched the horses and the blue lights disappear and then rode back and looked for the dead drones. He rode carefully along on horseback and wished he had Old Blue with him to find the small machines. Then he saw a blue light flashing in the grass ahead. He dismounted and found the drone, one rotor still turning. The machine had a camera pod suspended beneath it, a central processor compartment with an antenna, and what looked like a half-inch-diameter tube projecting forward and down and lined up with the camera. The tube was bent midway along its length, and a three-inch-diameter cylinder was attached to the rear end of the tube. The whole drone was about three feet across without the rotors that were nearly a foot in diameter themselves. Hardy found the second drone by its blue light.

He carried them over to Hickok, who had just concluded a radio conversation.

"What you got there? They look pretty big."

"I turned one off using a switch I found on the bottom side." Hardy held up one of the machines for Hickok to examine.

"What do you make of this attachment?" He pointed to the half-inch-diameter tube.

"Not sure, but it looks like one of those dart guns the wildlife guys use for shooting bears—ones that are causing trouble at trash dumps in town." He lifted the drone for a closer look. "Maybe they use that to drug the horses and make them easier to handle."

"That's pretty clever if it works right. You'd need fewer hands if you could sedate them." Hardy rubbed his chin as he thought about it. "But horses are pretty sensitive to drugs. They could die if you give 'em too heavy a dose. It can put them out for good."

"Yeah, vets gotta be real careful with anesthetic when they operate." Hickok swore under his breath. "I'd like to get my hands on these bastards for treating my wild horses like that. They could kill them just trying to capture them."

"Well, let's see what we can do about that." Hardy dropped the drones on the ground and saddled up. "Let's see if we can catch up to those guys."

Hickok said, "I got ahold of the sheriff. His name's Buck Johnson. He's getting his deputies and drivin' up to Skunk Canyon to cut these guys off before they can get out on Highway 372 that runs up the west side of White Mountain. I'm assuming these guys would load the animals on trailers and haul them down the valley to the highway. Then they'd probably head north to Montana or over into Idaho. They'd avoid Rock Springs and Green River."

"You know the way, Bill. I'll follow." Hardy reined his horse around. "Let's ride."

They rode north to where the mustangs had dropped into the head of Skunk Canyon, a long valley that trended west. They rode carefully in the dark, letting the horses pick their way through the unseen ground. In an hour, they came upon the remains of an abandoned ranch. They could see light down below, where several trucks were pulled up side by side in an arc so that their headlights illuminated a makeshift corral. Two additional construction klieg lights powered by a generator added light to the scene.

There were nearly two dozen horses in the corral, some strutting nervously around and some just standing there. Four men were riding on horseback, moving mustangs around in the corral. A man was standing by the side of the corral with a dart rifle. He seemed to be shooting at the spirited animals, probably with darts, tranquilizing them. A large cattle trailer attached to a pickup truck was backed up to a loading ramp at the corral gate. The horsemen were driving mustangs up the loading ramp and into the trailer. Another truck and trailer were parked down the road already loaded and ready to leave the valley.

"The horses in the first trailer might be ones from last night. The ones captured tonight are in the corral, by the looks of it." Hickok peered through his binoculars. "We'll let the loaded trailer go. The sheriff should be able to stop them. That leaves about eight or nine men for us to deal with."

Hardy followed Hickok as he rode lower down the slope in the darkness and headed toward the road below the loading activity. Before long, he pulled up and they both dismounted. Hickok unpacked his long gun, the .30-06, and attached his telescopic sight to it. Then he handed his shotgun to Hardy and had him fill his pockets with shells of birdshot. Hardy had his Ruger with him too.

"OK. Here's what we're gonna do. We'll leave the horses here out of harm's way and move in closer on foot. Then we'll find some cover by those rocks over there, and I'll take out their klieg lights with this baby." He patted his rifle. "When I start shooting, they're goin' to get riled up, so you take out the headlights on the vehicles and anyone who starts shootin' up at us." Hickok stared hard at Hardy in the moonlight. "I know you know about killin' a man, so there's that. But don't shoot anyone who's not shooting at us. It'll be self-defense anyway."

"You got it." Hardy was dead serious as he spoke. "These guys look like they're armed to the teeth, so be careful. I see at least one AK-47 down there." He pointed to a man standing guard on the road beyond the trucks. "He's their point man on the road."

"OK. I'll keep an eye on him right after I take out the lights."

"Hope they don't have night vision too," Hardy said dryly.

"All we gotta do is keep 'em tied up until Buck gets here with his boys." Hickok nodded to the shotgun. "What scares me are the damn drones. If they get those in the air after us, they got some kind of infrared sensors or vision on them. You keep an eye out for the little blue lights and take the buggers out fore they stick us with one of those darts. The dose they got for slowing horses down would kill a man if it hit you."

They took up positions behind boulders about twenty feet apart and watched the men load horses onto the trailer. The animals were forced up the ramp and onto the trailer by two of the men on horseback. The mustangs staggered slowly as if drugged while the riders slapped them with straps or lengths of rope. One horse fell sideways off the loading ramp and flailed its legs to get up again. The men drove other horses past it into the trailer, leaving it lying there with its legs thrashing. The trailer pulled forward, and another truck backed a trailer up to the ramp.

The downed horse was in the way of the trailer, so one of the men threw a lariat around the horse's neck, wound the end of the rope around the pummel of his saddle, and then dragged the animal out of the way on its side. The horse was choking and resisted a short time before it stopped struggling. That was more than Wild Bill could stand to watch.

He jumped up and shouted at the top of his lungs, "Halt! What you are doing? You're under arrest." A few of the men heard his call but some did not.

He opened fire to get their attention.

Hickok shot out the klieg lights first, one at a time, until the only light remaining came from the truck headlights, and then Hardy began shooting those out. The sound of the commotion and horses screaming smothered the first shots, but as the lights shattered over their heads, the men realized that someone was shooting at them. They took cover and returned fire.

The guard on the road stood still, apparently listening for the source of the gunfire and watching for muzzle flashes. Then he turned and unleashed a volley of automatic weapons fire at Hickok's position. That lasted about ten seconds, until Hickok aimed at him and fired once. The man fell backward on the ground. By that time, the man who had dragged the horse pulled out a rifle and shot at Hickok as he rode up the slope. Hickok aimed at him center-chest and took him out; the man tumbled backward over the tail of his horse.

Hardy fired his rifle at the truck headlights one by one, as well as the windshields, making the men keep their heads down. He also shot out a couple of truck tires, figuring that the men couldn't go anywhere with flat tires. He made use of iron sights in the dark, so he wasn't as accurate as he would have liked. Then bullets zipped over his head, and he ducked behind the boulder to reload.

By now they had a real firefight on their hands, and the few horses that weren't drugged broke through the half-open gate where the trailers were being loaded. Soon those horses ran up the hill away from the gunfire and into the safety of darkness.

Hickok had dropped three men for sure and had two others pinned down behind a truck. Hardy fired his .308 and hit one man who had tried riding up on him on horseback, firing a pistol. Then two others on horseback disappeared into darkness on the down-valley side of the corral.

Hickok shouted to Hardy, "You keep dumping lead on the ones down there while I see where the riders are goin'." He pulled out his night vision glasses and spied on the riders. Sure enough, they were working their way around to a flanking position. Hickok moved to another location by a second boulder and watched the riders carefully. Then he sighted in on one rider when a cloud cleared off and the man was visible in the moonlight. Hickok fired.

Hardy emptied his weapon and had to sit back and reload again. Suddenly there was a whirring sound overhead. He heard something thump into the ground next to him and rolled over to where he had left the shotgun. He raised the weapon as a blue light appeared above him, then another. He lay on his back and fired four times. The drones tipped sideways, and one crashed upslope from him. The other one flew off.

Hardy kept an eye out above him but turned back and fired on the men below. During the two minutes he had been preoccupied with reloading and blasting drones out of the night sky, the rustlers in the valley had begun to scamper away. The truck pulling the trailer was creeping down the road with a load of horses. Two more men tried driving away in a truck with a flat tire. They limped along into the darkness in retreat. A loud report from Hickok's rifle told him the other man on horseback was no longer a threat.

Four more drones suddenly appeared above their heads, and Hardy lay on his back to shoot two of them. Then he rolled a couple of times to his left and unloaded his shotgun at the remaining machines. One more went down, but the last one homed in on him, and he had no shells left. It approached and shot a dart at him. He kept rolling as the machine hovered over him for a second dart shot.

Hickok saw the drone attack Hardy and stood up suddenly. He pulled out his pistol like lightning and fired two shots at the drone. The machine seemed to break in two before crashing to the ground. Then Hickok dropped for cover again and shouted over to Hardy, "I hate those damn things. But they make a good moving target for quick-draw practice." He chuckled as he shouted again. "I think we got 'em on the run."

Hardy couldn't laugh and simply looked up to see if there were any men left fighting below them. Seeing none, he crawled over to check that the drones were truly disabled and wouldn't pose any further danger. He switched off the ones he found.

Then the sound of sirens came from down valley, and they could see the blue-and-red glow of emergency lights on the canyon walls. They heard gunfire for a minute and then it stopped.

Suddenly there came the racking sound of a dirt bike engine, and they watched as a bike drove diagonally up the hill on the other side of the valley. The headlight illuminated the brush as it careened along, someone making an escape up the steep slope. Hickok took aim at the driver but held fire because the bike was already too far away for an effective shot. They watched the bike climb up, roar over the ridge crest, and disappear into the night.

"I wonder who the hell that was. Sure can ride that thing," Hickok said, disappointed. "I could just make out green and silver colors on the bike, that's all. Well, one got away."

They sat in the dark and reloaded their weapons just in case it wasn't over. The moonlight came and went as clouds drifted overhead. Police cars roared up the road, and Hickok radioed his position to Buck and his deputies.

"No sense in them mistaking us for the bad guys." Hickok chuckled. "I've had enough fun for one night."

***

The next morning, Hardy and Hickok were back in Skunk Canyon after cleaning up at Hickok's home and catching a few hours' sleep. Hickok had ridden on horseback up to the ridge with a deputy to collect the two drones he had shot down the night before as evidence. Hardy had walked up the canyon slope and helped Deputy Dan Sutter find the remains of the drones Hardy had shot there. They located them, and the deputy marked the spot with a series of orange-numbered plastic cones so that they could collect the evidence after photographing the scene.

"You boys sure had a hell of a fight up here." Sutter waved his hand at all the shell casings on the ground. "Hey, what the hell is this?" He pointed to a tranquillizer dart that was sticking in the ground, its needle in the dirt and the red-feathered tail standing up.

"Tranquilizer dart," Hardy said. "They tried shooting us with darts from those quadcopter drones." He reached down to pick it up.

"Wait," Sutter said. "Better leave it and mark it as evidence. It might still be dangerous." He dropped a plastic cone next to it. "There's another one." In all they found five darts either sticking up in the dirt or lying on top of the ground. Sutter said, "Our lab guys had better come up here and collect this stuff. We'll just mark it."

When they finished marking everything, the area looked like an urban crime scene, with three dozen orange cones clustered where the fight had taken place. They walked down to the corral and the sheriff's vehicles parked on the road.

Sheriff Buck Johnson called them over for a talk just as Hickok rode up on a compact sorrel horse. Johnson was a tall, fiftysomething, weather-beaten man who looked like he had stepped right out of a John Wayne movie set. He had a new white Stetson Skyline hat on his head and a crisp, snap-up Western shirt over a pair of worn but clean Levi's and snakeskin boots. He looked like Western justice had looked since the days of the early cowboys.

When they were all gathered around him, Johnson spoke. "We found two other horses dead near the corral. Looks like they died from too much sedative. Plus this one they dragged last night." He spat on the ground next to a man's body bag that a coroner's office worker had just labeled. It contained the body of the man who had dragged the animal and who was one of the first to die at the shootout.

"Son of a bitch should have been dragged on a rope himself for mistreating an animal like that." He jabbed his finger at the body. "Can't blame you for pluggin' the guy, Bill. I would have done the same."

There was silence for a minute as they looked around them. Several other body bags lay on the ground among the evidence markers and shell casings.

"It'll take the evidence team a while to document all this. And I'll need you two to make statements as soon as you can while your memories are fresh. That will let us tie it all up for one hell of a report."

"Sure, Buck. Whenever you want." Hickok put a plug of snuff under his lip and nodded his head. "What else do ya need?"

"We caught five men last night as they left the canyon. Shot two dead before they surrendered. One of them told us they were hired to load up mustangs that someone else would herd down here into the canyon. He said he met the man who hired them only once—some Chinese guy with a lot of money he was throwing around. He said another Chinese guy operated those drones, but he didn't speak much English so he kept to himself. He said he was the one who lit out of here on the dirt bike last night." Johnson took his hat off and ran his fingers around the rim after he brushed some dust off it.

"But he got away clean?" Hardy asked.

"We asked around town," Johnson continued, "and found out that three Chinese-looking gentlemen were bunked at the Desert Inn over in Green River for the last five days. They had dirt bikes on a trailer when they packed up and left town before daylight this morning."

"Where'd they go?" Hickok looked angry.

"Well, that's what I'd like to know." Johnson shook his head. "Maggie at the front desk said they had a lot of electronic stuff with them, and they drove a green Yukon with Montana plates, probably a rental."

"You put out a BOLO on the car?" Hickok asked.

"Yeah, but they could be long gone by now. Probably headed for Montana . . . Canada even."

"Shit," Sutter said. "Well, they'll get caught sooner or later."

Buck looked Hardy up and down. "I just heard from the Montana State Patrol that they caught up with two horse trailers on Highway 89 north of Livingston. They arrested the drivers of the trucks pulling them. They were trying to get the horses across the border into Canada. They already had some documentation on the horses—papers like they were all purchased nice and legal."

He eyed Hickok. "The Montana people don't want anything to do with the horses. Got no facilities to hold 'em for evidence, they say. Probably just don't want any more mustangs to deal with in their state."

"So what happens to them?" Hardy asked.

Buck Johnson looked Hardy right in the eye. "How'd you two like to go on a road trip and bring our ponies back where they belong?"

***

Six hours later, Hardy, Hickok, and Deputy Sutter were all squeezed into the front seat of Hickok's Dodge truck driving east on I-90 in Montana. They had decided to take Hickok's rig and pick up the horses, bringing them south. Hickok and Sutter would drive the trucks and trailers back with the evidence while Hardy drove Hickok's pickup home. That way the evidence was always under control of the authorities, not a civilian. Sutter would sign for the horses and vehicles, which were being held in Sweet Grass County where Big Timber was located. The arrested men were being handled separately through channels to get them back for trial in Wyoming. Horses requiring care by professionals were transferred directly to the Sweet Grass sheriff's office by this personal transaction.

"According to the Montana folks, these two trailers we're getting are the first two loads of horses the thieves captured and shipped north. They were headed to an airport outside Calgary where they would turn them over to others and drive back to Wyoming. So these trailers probably contain Black Storm's herd," Hickok explained. "I sure hope they're OK after being boxed up all this time."

"Why didn't the troopers let them out of the trailers?" Hardy asked. "Seems cruel to keep them packed in all this time."

"I wondered about that too," Sutter said.

"They apparently weren't sure what to do with them. Some lawyer told them they should worry about liability or some dumb shit like that." Hickok started to spit tobacco juice out the window but decided against it. "Once they were out of the trailers, they would need to be examined by a vet to see if they could travel again. State troopers have no place to do that. If they got loose, they didn't have horses for rounding them up again. Go figure."

"Sounds kinda bureaucratic," Hardy commented.

"At least we're getting them back, no questions asked." Hickok checked his gas gauge and frowned. "We better pick up some go-juice at this little station here. I'll pull over, and we can gas up before we get to the troopers' office."

"We got time for a burger at the diner next door too," Sutter said.

Hickok pulled into the station next to a gas pump, and they all climbed out of the truck. There was a diner attached to the station and a small motel named the Trail's End next door. Hardy stretched his legs and cramped muscles.

"You guys go get us a table for lunch. I'll fill 'er up first." Hickok started pumping gas.

Hardy and Sutter shuffled into the diner and took a table right by the front window. They sat down, and a friendly middle-aged waitress came over with menus and a pot of hot coffee right away.

"You boys want coffee?" She started pouring before they could respond.

"Yes, ma'am. Thank you." Sutter beamed up at the woman. "We got one more coming too."

As they sipped their coffee, a shiny black Toyota 4Runner raced past the window next to their table and continued toward the motel. It didn't stop at the front office but went around the corner to the back of the motel.

Hardy didn't pay much attention, but Sutter commented, "The man must be in a hurry." He added, "Enterprise rental. One of those hybrid models—supposed to be great on mileage."

When Hickok came in, they all ordered burgers and fries. Hardy excused himself to use the restroom and walked toward the back of the restaurant. He found the men's room and took care of business. He washed his hands at the sink that was located below an open window to ventilate the room. As he stood up and dried his hands on paper towels, he had a view of the back side of the motel.

"I'll be damned," he said.

Right there behind the motel was a dark-green Yukon truck hitched to a trailer carrying two green Kawasaki dirt bikes. They were covered in dust, but the green and silver trim on them stood out clearly. The 4Runner he had just seen pull around the motel was parked right next to the Yukon. Three men were busy moving black plastic cases of gear and a few storage boxes from the Yukon into the 4Runner.

Hardy dropped the paper towel into the trash bin and ran out to the diner. At their table, he said, "Guys, you won't believe it, but they're here—the rustlers—right next door at the motel."

"No way," Sutter said.

The three stepped outside. Hickok walked over to his truck and got his Colt and holster. As he strapped it on he said, "How do you want to do this, Dan? It's your call."

Sutter checked his sidearm, a Glock 9mm. "Bill, see if you can pull your rig around and block their exit on the far side of the motel." He looked at Hardy and reconsidered. "Maybe you should do that instead so that Bill can be on the ground with his hands free . . . if you know what I mean." He paused. "I'll call the local 911 for help once we have them bottled up."

Hardy did as he was told and drove the Dodge to the end of the motel where a small alleyway allowed vehicles access to the rear of the motel. A cyclone fence that enclosed the motel property ran on the far side of the alley, limiting the space along the side of the building. He parked the truck, got out, and walked back to the front of the motel out of the line of fire if anything happened.

Hickok walked forward and took up a position directly in front of his truck where he could see the men transferring their load between vehicles. It looked like they had just finished. Sutter came around the other side of the motel near the gas station and took up a position next to the corner.

They heard police sirens approaching. *Ooo-be, ooo-be.* A screech of tires on asphalt told them that the sheriff's department had arrived. One cruiser skidded to a stop behind Hickok's truck and another stopped by the motel office. A deputy jumped out of his car, hand on his sidearm, and asked Hardy what he was doing there.

"I'm not the problem. Sutter and Hickok are around back where the rustlers are packing up," Hardy said.

"OK. I'm Deputy Moontree. Don't move." The deputy, a Native American with coal-black hair, sidestepped around the corner to assess the situation. Hardy followed him around the motel where he talked to Hickok.

The sirens spooked the three rustlers, who threw the last of their gear into the 4Runner and piled into it. The driver revved the engine and spun the tires, kicking up a spray of gravel as he backed out of the parking space. Then he gunned it, racing to the end of the motel just as Hickok and Moontree stepped out around the corner to face him. The driver hit the brakes and backed up, tires spitting gravel to the other end of the motel where Sutter stood in a firing stance with his Glock trained on the 4Runner. The driver skidded to a halt when he saw there was no alley on that end of the motel. Hardy heard the men in the vehicle shouting at one another in Chinese about what to do next.

The driver revved the engine. He hesitated a moment and then turned the 4Runner toward Hickok's vehicle and the men positioned there. He floored the gas and picked up speed fast.

Both Hickok and Moontree raised their weapons and began firing at the windshield of the 4Runner as it roared at them. Neither man stepped aside to get out of the way of the raging vehicle. They landed round after round on the glass, and the window showed each hit with a spatter of fractured glass. Suddenly the 4Runner veered to the right and rammed into the cyclone fence, tearing a gap in it and knocking posts down, but it stalled as it was caught in a huge steel net of fencing.

The driver jumped out of the car and pulled a handgun from under his jacket. He didn't stand a chance. Both Hickok and Moontree fired twice. The man fell to the ground, getting off only one shot before he died. The other men in the 4Runner began shouting, "No shoot! No shoot!" They crawled out of the vehicle with their hands in the air.

***

The next few days flashed by for everyone involved in the mustang rustling investigation. The two Chinese men who were captured in Montana refused to tell the police more than a few basic facts, but even that information ended when a Chinese-speaking attorney showed up from California. Someone in China wanted the men left alone and put up barriers to any further questioning.

Buck Johnson met Hardy and Hickok for lunch the third day after they returned to Wyoming with the stolen mustangs. The three of them sat in Woody's Burger Paradise in Green River. Old

Blue was allowed into the restaurant and lay under their table as they ate. Hardy dropped a few bites of burger as a treat for his friend.

"The dead man who was the leader and the one who hired the local talent provided us with some information indirectly," Johnson said between bites of an egg salad sandwich. "It turned out he was a retired Chinese intelligence officer who was working freelance for some of the most powerful and wealthy men in China. We think the other two men had similar backgrounds."

"I heard that the head of the American rustlers, the local talent, was ready to talk. Is that right, Buck?" Hickok asked.

"Yeah." Buck sipped his beer. "That guy, Rufus Simms Murphy, wanted to cut a deal and reduce his list of charges. It's real long—rustling, attempted murder, and other things. So the federal prosecutor cut him a deal, and we got his story."

"That's good news. How'd he get into this mess anyway?"

"He was contacted about three months ago to line up a team of rustlers for rounding up and transporting the stolen horses to Canada. He selected Skunk Canyon as the corral site, built the temporary enclosure, and set up all the other equipment they would need. He rounded up black-hat cowboys from all over the criminal West for the job. He had a lot of contacts because of his past work."

They all ordered another beer to finish washing down their meals. "The leader told Murphy he wanted too many men. That the Chinese guy had a way of collecting the horses off the mountain if Murphy could just deal with them once they were delivered to Skunk Canyon." Johnson sipped his beer. "Apparently, the Chinese had experimented with herding animals with drones and planned on bringing the mustangs down to the corral. They've developed a way of controlling multiple drones at once as a swarm. One man flew them from the top of Pilot Butte, and he passed off control once the horses moved more than seven miles north. Another drone pilot then took over and brought the horses to the canyon and down to the corral. Pretty slick operation." Johnson finished his sandwich and looked around for their server.

"And we know the rest," Hickok said. "We brought the horses back and put them in the BLM holding facility for a few days of observation. You know—to be sure the drugs had worked their way out of their systems. They all seem to be just fine and are ready for release on White Mountain. You'll all have to come out and watch in a couple of days."

"Yeah," Hardy said. "I hope that Lori and Andy can be here for that." Blue woofed at that and then lay down again, overwhelmed by food smells.

"But why did they steal the horses at all? There had to be a bigger plan," Hardy said.

"Murphy told us that he had heard from the Chinese guy that he worked for a very rich and important man in China who loved the American West and had read all the old writers—Zane Gray, Louis L'Amour, Larry McMurtry—you know. Anyway, he wanted to start his own herd of wild horses somewhere in western China." He stopped and rolled his eyes. "I know— bizarre idea, right? But that's how it all began."

"Wow, that's really out there. If the guy was that crazy about mustangs, he probably could have arranged to get an export license. Could have done it all real legal." Hardy blew out some air and shook his head.

"Money makes some people think they can do anything," Hickok said as he stood up from the table. "Hey, I gotta go get some work done. You guys take care."

Johnson and Hardy shook hands and left the restaurant. Old Blue followed dutifully behind his friend.

***

One week after Hardy witnessed the drones chasing the mustangs and the rustling was discovered, Hickok, Johnson, Sutter, and Hardy Harris stood on the dirt road that serviced the south side of White Mountain and led to Pilot Butte. Lori Phillips and her son, Andy, were there as well, and Old Blue was sitting right between Hardy and Andy. It was getting dark after delays had slowed down the release of the horses back to their wild pasture on the mountain.

The whole affair worked out just right for Lori and Andy to be there and to join Hardy for a few days of camping and wild horse viewing. They were both enjoying the outdoor adventure and were excited to see the mustangs returned to their home in the wild.

They were all standing along the road, waiting as the sun sank lower in the sky and the colors began illuminating the clouds on the western horizon. Four trailers of horses were lined up, with men standing by the tailgates to let the horses free. The spectators were anticipating a unique scene as the mustangs were released.

Hickok signaled and a wrangler dropped the gate on the first trailer, lowering it quickly but not letting it bang on the ground. As soon as the gate hit the dirt, the first horse bolted out onto the road, soon followed by the rest of the cargo. This was the western herd, the second lot captured by the rustlers, and within moments their stallion took charge and led his family away to the west, at first along the road and then breaking into a trot in the tall grass. The horses all had their ears pricked up and their heads held high in the air as they whinnied and moved toward the western shoulder of the mountain.

The second trailer was opened, and the last herd to be rustled came carefully out, smelled the air, and moved off toward the horizon. Within minutes, the horses were mere specks on the grassland.

The wrangler opened the third trailer, the one that contained half of Black Storm's herd. The horses from that trailer ran out, having been away from their home the longest, sniffing the air and the smell of freedom. They seemed to recognize where they were immediately, but they moved only a short distance into the tall grass, away from the humans, and waited. The mares with their foals stood with their family as whinnies and snorts came from the fourth trailer where their leader pawed the gate.

Finally, the wrangler lowered the gate on the last trailer, and the huge black stallion, Black Storm, sprang out, snorting and bellowing loudly. Then all the others from the trailer rushed out onto the roadway, sniffing the air and whinnying with apparent joy. The big stallion reared up and then walked among his herd as if to check that they were all there. He snorted and nipped at a few of the horses, forming them into a tighter group.

The sun had begun to set in the west, with deep-orange light flooding the landscape. Black Storm circled his herd and moved them off the road, away from the crowd. He stopped and looked at the assembled humans. He whinnied again and trotted over toward them as if to see who they were and to assess whether his herd was in danger. He came closest to Hickok's truck, perhaps one he had seen many times before, and snorted when Hickok raised his hand and called out. "Go home, Blackie. You're safe now. Go home."

The black horse whinnied, nodding his head up and down several times as if he understood. Then, in an instant, he spun around and trotted toward his herd. He issued a single scream and then broke into a slow gallop, with his companions following behind. He ran west into the setting sun. Hardy could almost feel the great sense of freedom the animals exhibited in their alert and carefree behavior.

"Wow!" Andy said, and everyone laughed as the horses moved away. "That was beautiful."

The mustangs ran west toward a low ridge, an extension of Pilot Butte that reached out to the south. As the horses crossed the ridge, they were silhouetted against the setting sun as the final red flares of light shot across the mountain. They disappeared over the crest of the ridge for a moment but then a single horse reappeared, as if he were looking back at Hardy and the others. It was Black Storm. He reared up into the sky, backlit by the red of the sun, and pawed the air as he emitted one final scream for the night.

Old Blue began to howl in his own version of joy. *Baroo! Baroo!*

And then Black Storm was gone.

Her Side of the Story

The funeral took place in the veterans' section of the local cemetery on a sunny afternoon in November. Sergeant George Miller was a marine veteran of the Second World War, having served in the Pacific Theater of Operations and been involved in battles on Iwo Jima and other island hellholes. He received a Purple Heart for being stabbed with a bayonet by a Japanese soldier on one of those islands, and he was proud to tell friends that he had the bayonet to show for it. The Japanese soldier had not come out of the confrontation well and so forfeited the weapon after George shot him.

For many years George didn't talk about the war much, and when he did, it was with only a few friends who he thought might not judge him too harshly. He was a quiet man by nature.

Because of his service to the country, George was accorded a gravesite with his fellow marines and an honor guard ceremony. Several people from the town nearby, as well as friends and acquaintances who had known him over the years, turned out to pay their last respects. Among them were Victor, who had been his friend for most of his life, and Norman, who knew him from his work on the reservation.

Hardy Harris knew George from a few encounters at the Veterans Affairs office in town. He liked George's spirit and sense of humor. So he attended the quiet ceremony to pay respects to a fellow marine and a man who had served his country well. He brought with him his best tail-wagging friend, Old Blue, his basset hound. They sat near the rear of the array of folding chairs that had been set out for the graveside service, only a few of them occupied by other mourners.

Victor was a Southern Ute who grew up on the reservation with George and who George had told of his many trials through life, during the war and during his long years with his deceased wife, Millie, and their only child, Ray, also deceased. Norman worked on the reservation at the post office and knew George from their many conversations about the weather and life in general. Norman and Victor were the only people who George had ever shown his bayonet scar to, except for his wife and child.

Unfortunately, George had no family left alive, and so Victor felt that he was the only close personal friend there to represent George's interests. He felt sadness for the old fellow as well as guilt that he had not gone to visit George more frequently. If he had, maybe there was something he could have done to help him during his last days.

For these reasons, he felt he should help preserve George's memory by taking in his few belongings, such as the bayonet and the burial flag that now draped the pine coffin at the graveside. He had asked Norman about the flag, and Norman told him that if he sat at the first chair at the head of the coffin, that the honor guard would place it in his hands at the conclusion of the ceremony. So when the service began, he made his way to the front chair.

Just then, there was a commotion toward the back as a short, gray-haired woman of many years pushed her way forward to the side of the gravesite. She attempted to throw herself on the coffin, which was now suspended over the grave. Luckily, the leader of the honor guard intercepted her before she stepped into the open pit during her emotional display.

Victor stepped forward and addressed her in friendly tones.

"Ma'am, you got to be careful and not fall in the open hole. Why don't you sit here by me and watch the ceremony."

Instead, she knelt by the grave and bent down in loud prayer in Shoshonean, the ancient language of the Southern Ute Tribe, followed by loud weeping that immediately drew sympathy from the surrounding mourners. But between all of them, in the ensuing delay and murmured conversations, not one of them knew who the woman was.

The presiding minister began the ceremony, as planned. He spoke kind words and praised George for his service and his life in the community, then the music played and the honor guard fired three volleys of seven rounds each. At the end the marines removed the flag from the coffin and carefully folded it in the traditional triangular package. Their leader marched over to Victor in the first chair and handed him the flag.

A howl of pain went up from the old woman as she reached for the flag, tugging at it as Victor tried to hold on. She was half-mad and weeping as she pulled.

She said in broken English, "It's mine. He was mine." She yanked so hard that she drew Victor sideways out of his chair and he fell onto the ground, letting go of the flag. The woman looked around and then began to run away with the banner.

She happened to run directly into the county deputy who was overseeing traffic for the ceremony. He held on to her and brought her back to the gravesite, where Victor tried to extract the flag from her clutches.

The minister came over and spoke in Spanish to the woman, asking her to settle down so that they could talk. He also asked Victor to hang on to the flag for the time being. Then he told her to tell him her name because no one there knew who she was.

And this is what she said.

"I am Maria. I know George many years. I clean his house after Millie die. But we more than friends, much more. It began with him joke with me, and I cook him lunch sometimes. Then my husband die and I was alone." She stopped and looked around at the funeral party.

The minister said, "So you're Maria. George mentioned you to me as a friend."

"Then George and me spend much time together, and I stay with him at night sometimes. Then all the time. I like his new wife, but not wife. We very happy. I work very hard cleaning houses so we can live together. Now he gone and I have nothing of George. I have nothing at all."

She looked from the minister to Victor. "I wanted to have something for remember him. But house locked now and I cannot get something. I wanted *bandera*—you call flag. Something of him, something good for good memories. Can I have from George?" She looked pleadingly at Victor.

Victor smiled at her as he began to understand. The minister put a reassuring hand on her shoulder.

Victor looked at the woman and said, "I've heard of you, Maria. George mentioned a Maria but didn't say much about you. I knew you were friends but not that you lived with him. He was a quiet old cuss that way and played things close to the vest sometimes." He hesitated but then looked kindly at Maria. "Maybe you should have his flag of honor. I think it would be right."

Victor carefully placed the folded flag in Maria's hands.

She smiled and hugged the flag close.

Talkeetna Blues

The woman on a tall roan horse rode up to me and said, "Have ya seen a yella dog? A big one with black in his face?"

Her tired gray eyes peered out from a lined, weather-tanned face that was framed by faded blonde hair and topped by a worn black Stetson that had clearly seen better days. The torn, faded Levi jacket and slacks, and even her aging ride, spoke of better times in the past. "He generally runs this way when he jumps the fence."

"I saw some dogs go around the corner a while ago but didn't see a yellow one," I said. "Wasn't really focused on it, ya know?" This was true. I wasn't really focused on anything at the moment.

I took a swig of my warm Coke and watched the horse and woman slump away down the gravel road toward the turn at the general store. The sounds of the onset of a dogfight around the corner caught my attention next. The woman called out, "Nicky?" and then set her reluctant ride to maximum warp speed—a trot. She disappeared around the corner, concerned but hopeful.

I was killing time, sitting on a bench in front of McNulty's Store on Main Street, watching a cloud of fluffed-out cottonwood seeds drift down the road, like a barrage of tiny parachutes. My intimate exposure to tasty ale hours before still made it difficult to focus on individual parachutes. But I enjoyed the impressionistic whole that surrounded me in the late afternoon sun.

The street was finally coming back to life after the extended convulsion of Midsummer Eve. Kids in ragged clothes rode rusty bikes up and down the street shoulder. Tourists gawked at stylized shops and quaint settings. Climbing wannabes strutted up and down the street wearing reflective glacier goggles and Vibram-soled boots, stopping to stare west at the mountains and clouds on occasion. Pickup trucks plied the street, some old, some new, but all with at least one dog in the back. Drivers stopped in the middle of the road to greet passing amigos going the opposite direction, and the dogs in back of each truck addressed each other noisily. Bent-up Datsuns and Escorts conveyed newly arrived youth and, of course, their dogs on aimless trips to the river and back.

An occasional tour bus cruised through town, spewing black diesel fumes in its wake. Gray-haired or balding gents with their blue-haired wives peered attentively out the windows, as their tour guide lectured over the bus's PA system. And here and there, victims and survivors of last night's reverie drifted tentatively along the side of the road, generally keeping out of the direct sunlight, ready to give life another try at their favorite watering hole.

The action last night had been down by the river, on the broad sand and cobble terrace that serves as a beach. People had pulled up pickups, trailers, and even a few rafts to sit in or on as encampments formed around bonfires and kegs of beer. Someone had set out a flatbed trailer to serve as a stage for the band. Power cords had extended two hundred yards through the alders to a cabin owned by an émigré named Vladimir and had powered the electronics for the show. The payment of a few bottles of good vodka each year brought Vladimir back to youthful memories of Ukrainian summers. As the sun dipped just below the horizon, the sky had dimmed but never went dark.

The party had swayed onward into the next morning, then sort of fizzled out as the revelers had fallen asleep or retreated to more comfortable quarters for romance. Brave souls, who had ventured into the bushes for a quickie, were ravaged by mosquitoes that sucked at least a pint of blood from each participant. Others had simply fallen over where they sat or were hauled away by their friends. One couple had slept peacefully in their raft until morning, a thoughtful stranger having covered their naked bodies with a Hudson Bay blanket.

I had met a lady during the night, a real beauty. She had introduced me to Ice Axe Ale, a tasty brew that had twice the alcohol content of ordinary beer. It was so named for the sneaky, latent headache that felt like your limbic brain had been cleaved by an ax blade. After several pints I had felt really good and could tell that my arcane humor was appreciated by all. The party continued on as the sun arced behind the distant Alaska Range.

The woman and I had danced most of the night, both sufficiently impaired to just sway with the sonic throb near the stage. Our attempts at dazzling and artistic expression were apparently lost on the lowbrows who competed for space on the open sand. To them we may have appeared to be two unstable legs of a teetering stool, but we knew at the time that we were the trendsetters of the scene.

Sometime that night, as we had smooched behind the band's van, my hand under her blouse and her bottom squirming in my lap, she whispered hoarsely, "My husband is coming!"

My response to this information was staged in a series of slow-motion realizations. First, I recorded the news on a higher language plane that seemed incongruent with the last several hours of companionship that Angie and I had shared. Then on a hormonal level, for unclear reasons, adrenaline began to flood my already overtaxed, testosterone-flushed system. This had created an enhanced state of sensory confusion and the beginning of an awareness that something bad was going to happen very soon. My neural pleasure centers were still anticipating ecstasy as my limbic brain began to shoot warning signals to my sluggish motor system. All this chemical stimulation and neural firing had come on slowly, even though only seconds had passed.

Too late, I had uttered, "What husband?" just as my lady friend twisted to one side and hit the ground at an acute angle. My hand still clutched thin air as a dark, subrectangular object had filled my entire range of vision. There had been no sensation of pain as the dark object appeared several more times, as it was applied with ruthless energy to my soon to become featureless face.

Gradually, pain had replaced all other senses, and I slumped into an amorphous heap near the van's rear wheel. A loud, raspy voice bathed me in a string of coarse epithets, some combinations of which I had not heard before. Some fancy footwork ended the session as darkness overtook me.

I lost track of time.

Later I was immersed in a warm, wet place as alternating pleasure and pain gradually seeped into my subconscious. In confusion, I somehow still anticipated some sexual favor as a tongue ardently bathed my aching flesh in juicy kisses. Trying to return the passion, I leaned into the warm embrace and felt as though I were flying in space. A sharp pain brought all this to an end as I lay on my back and then fell from the sofa. Vladimir's dog, Max, barked excitedly and then continued to lap at my bruised but colorful features.

"Ah! So he is alive!" Vladimir came forward with a cup of miner's coffee. "See if you can drink this. It will make you strong!" The coffee contained enough whiskey to quell some of the pain in my head, equal parts hangover and damaged tissue.

After being sick, washing up in Vlad's outdoor basin, and eating an egg sandwich, I began to feel like I might survive. Vladimir told me that the band had found me puking on their drive wheel and had brought me to his cabin rather than call the cops. It seems that given the levels of assorted legal and illegal substances in their possession, they had been real Boy Scouts to not just leave me in the muskeg. Vlad said that I could have done worse if my opponent had landed more of his punches on me instead of the now-dented panel van. I took some satisfaction that the fist had gotten its share of abuse. He dropped me at my home, the hostel, such as it was, and I recovered for a few hours.

So here I am, sitting in the sun, feeling warm and lucky. Just bidding my time until the West Buttress Saloon opens for the evening. It won't be long before I can sip a cool Axe and watch the clientele come out for refreshment. It will turn out all right. I'll have to watch out for an hombre with a bandaged hand. And who knows? Maybe the love of my life will walk through the door, come to my side, and smother me with kisses.

It can happen! After all, I'm still an optimist.

Night Breeze: The Bear

Something was not quite right. Brady had slipped out of the screen door, being careful not to slam it as he did so. He stood there in the dark, his back against the wall of his log cabin, as he let his eyes and other senses adjust to the quiet outdoors. He had thought he heard a scraping noise while lying in bed, just on the verge of slumber. He was not sure what it was, only that it did not belong here at night in his little corner of the forest.

He closed his eyes and let his hearing extend out into the night air. He heard the wind blow through the aspens that stood across the grassy meadow that he called his front yard. He smelled the night air, the moisture of spring starting to come to this level of the mountains as snow continued to melt during the warm spring night. He heard almost no animal noises tonight, unusual in a forest where small and large creatures normally grazed or moved about at this time. He opened his eyes again, now that they had had time to penetrate the darkness.

It was a full moon night, warm and peaceful, with a partly cloudy sky, clouds drifting across the moon frequently, pulling a drape over the light and sinking the landscape into greater darkness as the clouds passed. Just then, a cloud crossed the moon, and the view of the meadow went dark.

Then he heard the noise again. It was a very quiet sound, like wet paper being crumpled and then torn. It came from the detached garage down near the creek that provided his water supply here in the Colorado mountains. The wind blew sounds around on a quiet evening like this, and the whispered scraping drifted in from different directions. The bubbling of the stream was close now and then farther away. The scraping sound seemed to come from the garage and then from the trees across the meadow.

Brady crossed the porch during one of the periods when the clouds covered the moon so that he would not be seen moving in the night. He walked in his moccasins, creating only the faint sound of his weight on the wood deck of the porch. Then he descended the few steps to the grass and walked along next to the gravel path rather than on it. He headed for the garage. The wind blew the sound of the water to him before he got there.

He approached the small manway door to the garage, being careful not to make any noise. A scrape arose from inside the building, and as he drew nearer, he could detect the sound of cardboard being torn and the noises of an animal eating something with relish. He thought it might be one of those damn raccoons that had broken into his food supply before. But you never knew what you might encounter out here. He approached the door from the hinge side so that he could push it open with his left hand. He had never liked that the door opened inward; it exposed him too much before he could see inside. In any case, he noticed that the door was ajar and something had obviously pushed its way into the garage.

Brady peered through the partly open door to see if there was any movement. He brought his .45-caliber Colt semiautomatic up in his right hand and eased the door open a bit more. He could see nothing in the complete darkness. Then a cloud revealed the light of the moon, and he took a quick breath. He saw someone or something standing upright in front of the window on the far wall, near the old Kenmore electric freezer. The figure saw him and turned his way. It stood nearly five feet tall and was quite burly, with projecting ears and a black snout that was plunged into a package of food of some sort. This was no raccoon. *It was a young bear!* Before he could react, the bear dropped to all fours and charged directly for the half-open door.

He tried to jump out of the way as the bear squeezed through the door, slamming it open in the process. Brady was knocked down and narrowly avoided being run over by the panicked creature as it turned and ran away from the garage, toward the stream.

Boy! That was close.

He laughed at himself for being surprised by a bear of all things. He got up off the ground and replaced his Colt in the waistband of his trousers. He looked after the retreating bear that was now thrashing its way through the underbrush along the creek. It must have just come out of hibernation and been extremely hungry after the long winter nap. Bears often broke into abandoned cabins in the spring looking for food. This guy was lucky and found the freezer with ice cream and other things inside.

Other things? he thought. *Better check on what's left in the freezer.*

He walked up to the largely shattered door and pushed on it to look inside. The moon was in shadow again, and he couldn't see a thing in the darkened interior. He stepped just inside the door—into the dark—and hesitated. He smelled something like musk. In an instant, he became aware that he was not alone. The hair on his neck rose straight up, then every hair on his body prickled as a sense of dread oozed through him. He felt a warm, moist breeze touch his face as the aroma of fruit and a nauseating, acrid stench filled the air in front of his face.

The clouds shifted off the moon, and its brightness flooded the garage with an eerie light. Brady glanced up to see the source of the hot, wet air, now only two feet from his face. In the dim light he could see only the whites of the eyes and the gleaming teeth of a huge bear that stood in front of him. It, too, had wondered what lurked in the dark on this unusual night.

The bear growled and leaned forward to bite its assailant. Brady had just enough time to raise his left arm for defense as he instinctively reached behind him for the pistol in his waistband. It did not matter. The bear shoved Brady's elbow into its mouth and bit down hard. So hard that the teeth went in deep and the bones were crushed in a sickening surge of pain. Brady nearly passed out at that moment, but deep down he knew that, in order to survive, he had to pull away from the overwhelming force of the bear. He didn't remember if he had even pulled the Colt's trigger to fire once. The bear continued its attack, shaking its powerful head, and Brady flopped about like a fish on a pike.

After a half minute of shaking Brady's body back and forth and sensing no further resistance, the bear released its jaws and swatted Brady on his left side. Then it bent down and bit one of his feet before finally striking him with the other paw, like a cat playing with a mouse. Brady stopped moving and lay there on the floor of the garage, no longer a threat. The bear moved out into the night.

***

Brady woke up and found himself under the workbench of the garage. The bear was gone, and he was left for dead or at least no longer of interest. *Could it have been the mother bear, also out of hibernation? It seemed awfully large for a mama black bear.*

He was in great agony. His elbow was numb, his left arm broken and exploding with pain. The blow delivered to his right side was not much better. His foot had been mauled by a couple of hefty bites from that huge jaw. He tried to get up by placing one hand on the floor and nearly lost consciousness. He pushed himself into a sitting position and realized he could not support any weight on his damaged foot. He unfastened his belt and used it to set a temporary tourniquet on his leg below the knee to staunch the bleeding. He needed to move, and he pulled himself up by using the workbench.

Brady looked over at the freezer. The latch had been broken and the lid flipped open. Frozen food had been strewn about by the hungry bears. He hobbled over to the freezer and closed it, placing a toolbox on top of the lid to hold it closed.

By the time he finished with the freezer, he realized he was getting light-headed from the loss of blood. He tried to walk to the garage door but slipped and nearly fell down. He looked at the floor and noticed that his leg was bleeding in spite of the tourniquet and that he was standing in a small pool of his own blood. His shirt was also beginning to drip blood from the saturated elbow wound. He knew that he had to get to his pickup truck where he kept his first aid kit. It was parked in front of the garage in the driveway.

He staggered out the now-mangled garage door, and the moon shone brightly to guide his way. In its light, he could see a wavy dark line on the ground leading away from the doorway toward the creek where the first bear had run and the second must have followed. He reached down to confirm it was a blood trail from the big bear. He had apparently gotten one round off and hit the animal.

Shit! Now I've got a wounded and angry bear on my hands. He would have to go after it in the forest tomorrow and finish it off, if he could follow the trail that far. Well, that was tomorrow and this was today.

Brady used a shovel as a crutch and made his way around the garage to the driveway. He was getting very tired now and started to think that maybe it would be quicker to drive to Dr. Wilson's cabin a mile away on dirt roads than to drive into town. He was getting weaker fast and was not sure he would be able to drive that far in his present condition. The doc could patch him up enough to stop the bleeding and get him into town after that. He pressed on toward the driveway and finally to his truck.

He made it to the driver's side door and held on to the side of the truck while he threw the shovel in the pickup's bed. He opened the door and reached behind the seat to retrieve the first aid kit. It was wedged in and he had to wrestle with it awhile to pull it free and place it on the seat of the truck. He did all this while standing next to the truck with the door open, and the effort had worn him out. He had to stop and catch his breath.

The moon went behind a cloud and darkness surrounded him. Then he heard the sound of gravel crunching behind him, and the hair on his neck stood up.

There's that musk smell again.

Night Breeze: Reprisal

Brady stood in front of Doc Wilson's house with his duffel bag. He walked across the lawn, half expecting his dog, Charlie, to come rushing out and besiege him on the grass. He climbed up the porch stairs slowly, being careful with his left foot. The pins in it were still settling in, and the doctor had said he would notice pain if he walked on it too soon. But he did so anyway, and it hurt like hell. He knocked on the screen door, expecting no answer. He dropped his bag on the porch deck and walked inside.

He knew his way to the kitchen, so he went in and helped himself to a cold one. Blue Moon. He twisted the top and took a long draw from the bottle. Not bad, but not his idea of a real brew. He would have to talk to Doc about stocking better beer and keeping his door locked. You never knew what critter was going to break in and make himself at home. He sauntered back out onto the porch and sat in the wooden swing to await Doc's return.

The mountains caught his attention first. It was summer now, June something, and the snow was still melting off the higher peaks. He wondered how his cabin had fared during the two months he had been gone. His eyes surveyed the scene before him, and his gaze locked onto the smashed fence post next to the driveway. The post and the first section of the white picket fence were knocked flat on the grass. Doc had apparently tried to straighten it by bracing the post up with a two-by-four, but it looked like hell. He had told Doc when he'd built it six years ago that he had put the post too close to the driveway. But he wouldn't listen to the voice of experience and low expectations.

Of course, Brady hadn't planned to be the one to demonstrate what would happen if someone came careening into it driving a pickup truck half out of control in the middle of the night.

Brady remembered that night clearly. Well—part of it anyway. He remembered how he smelled the musk scent again and just had time to climb into the cab of the truck before the bear had lunged. He had started the truck and backed out of the driveway at high speed. The headlights had just caught the tail end of the huge bear as it ran around the corner of the garage into the night. Apparently, it did not like trucks much.

He had driven down to Doc's place after he tightened the tourniquet on his leg. The pain was enough to keep him from passing out. He remembered roaring into Doc's driveway, splashing gravel all over and swerving to the right at the last minute to avoid rear-ending Doc's 4Runner. That was when he ran over the post and came to a stop on the lawn. The next thing he knew, there was a flashlight shining in his eyes, along with Doc's 9mm Berretta peering in through the side window that the bear had broken out. Doc had taken a look at the bloodied face and recognized it as his chess-playing neighbor and didn't shoot him for the rude awakening.

Doc had treated him like any other wounded warrior he had ever seen in combat and applied triage at the scene. He ran into the house and came back wearing a headlamp and carrying a first aid kit. His first action had been to throw a large plastic zip tie around the mangled left leg that the bear had treated like a chew toy. He cinched it up so tight that it caused his patient to come fully awake. Then he cut away the shirtsleeve to reveal a gory mass of blood and gristle that he could not treat in the field. He put a large gauze pad on it and taped it quickly before putting a second tourniquet of the plastic kind in place to stop blood loss there. He would rather have a one-armed chess opponent than a dead one.

With the blood loss under temporary control, Doc had used zip ties to attach two bags of saline to the rearview mirror and then spent way too long hunting for a vein to insert a needle. After a few tries, he tapped a vein and squeezed some volume into the rapidly draining body. He ran inside again to make a call and to tell his daughter, Julie, he had to go into town on an emergency.

Then he had used all his strength to push his patient across the bench seat of the truck so that he could get in and drive. In doing so, he pressed on Brady's bad arm and torso, and he came violently awake from the pain.

"What the hell are you doing, Doc? We should get in your car and go to the clinic," Brady seemed to say in his slurred speech.

Doc climbed into the driver's side and threw the idling truck into reverse to back off the lawn and out onto the road.

"Oh no, Brady! I'm not getting your blood all over my car seat. No way!"

Then he punched the old Ford hard and threw gravel all over the lawn as he raced for town.

Brady didn't remember the rest but had been told how Doc got him to the clinic, the only urgent care facility in sixty miles. It was not usually staffed at night except during hunting season. That was when they saw the majority of their trauma cases, mostly drunk hunters who fell into a campfire or shot themselves in the foot when they should have known better.

Dr. Wilson saved his life that night. After a quick evaluation, they called for a Flight for Life helicopter to come from Denver, where they could deal with these types of serious injuries.

That was two months ago, and the medical team at Saint Anthony's Hospital managed to repair the damage pretty well. Brady had pins in his foot and ankle but had no real trouble with the joint itself. His elbow had been a different story, since it had been mangled pretty badly. They said he was in good physical condition and that was the only reason he did not bleed to death. Plus he had an expert doctor, friend, and chess player who kept him alive.

He spent two weeks at Saint Anthony's before being transferred to the veterans' facilities on the other side of Denver for his rehab and final treatments. Doc had connections there and got him in right away, with none of their godforsaken waiting lists. In eight weeks, Brady was good to go, or at least he refused to stay under their care any longer. He had been in a VA hospital before in the old days and had not liked it one bit. He wanted to get home to his cabin in the mountains.

Doc Wilson drove up in his 4Runner as Brady pondered what he would do next at the cabin. Wilson carried two bags of groceries from the car to the kitchen and greeted his friend as he did so. His guest supervised as Wilson put away the groceries and beer that Brady thought was a more agreeable brand. Then they each took a bottle of Bass Ale and returned to the porch to talk and catch up on things.

"You grew a beard?" was the first comment out of Wilson's mouth. "What's a big lug like you going to do with a beard? Haven't you got enough hair on your head as it is?" He pointed his bottle in Brady's direction. "Julie's goin' to think you went all Paul Bunyan living up there in the woods by yourself." He chuckled as he stared at Brady's new growth. "Oh yeah, she'll comment for sure." Doc always made a fuss about hair, having a shiny dome as he did.

"Thought you'd like it, Doc."

"They told me you practically drained their blood bank in Denver. I don't know how you even pulled through. I didn't know you had so much blood in you." He glanced sideways at Brady. "What are you, a vampire or something?"

Brady laughed. It felt good to be around friends after his hospital stay.

"Well, I saw the bite on your elbow when we cleaned you up," Doc said, "and that was not from any female black bear, or any black bear at all that I've seen." He paused to sip his ale and look at the mountains. "It reminds me of some Grizzly bites I saw when I was living in Montana. For one thing the bite is too wide for a black bear." He took a slug of ale before continuing his discourse. "I wish I had made a mold of the bite and then we would have something to show the wildlife people. You know, some hunters have said they've seen a big grizzly here in the back side of the Gore Range, but they're not supposed to be this far south."

"So what do you want to take a photo for, the record or something?" Brady rolled up his shirtsleeve. "It's a beauty of a scar." That started a series of events going, and they wound up photographing the scar and taking measurements for Wilson's records, since he was the unofficial wildlife attack expert on the mountain. They also photographed the small scars from the claws when the bear had struck his arm.

That settled, they got more beers.

"So, Brady, I want you to stay here with me a couple of days instead of heading up to the cabin. You could take a little more time to get your strength back and your truck fixed before going home. You could have the spare room, and we could catch up on chess and cards." He stopped talking and smiled at Brady. "But, in two days, my daughter, Julie, is coming back up with the kids, so I'll need the room after that."

"That reminds me. Where's Charlie? Did you get him OK the next day?" Brady asked about his dog's fate.

"I went up there that night with the sheriff to get him out of the bedroom where you locked him in. That was a smart move. Otherwise he might have got cut up trying to defend your sorry ass from the bear."

"Thanks, Doc." He looked around the porch. "So where's my dog?"

"Julie has him." Doc smiled at his friend. "And by the way, I had old One-Armed Joe go up the next day and replace that piece of shit you called a garage door. He'll send you a big bill, I'm sure, but what are friends for?"

"Thanks, you scoundrel. What happened to my truck?"

"I had Joe take it to get it repaired. The fender wasn't bad enough to replace from when you plowed into my fence. Those old F-150s can really take a beating, which is why you drive one, I suppose." He chuckled as he took another slug of beer. "But the seats were soaked with blood, and there is no getting that out of the cushions, so I had Joe take it over to Jimbo's for him to find you a replacement seat from some junker." He paused to eye Brady. "If you want to go for a drive, Jimbo left a message that he has a seat for you but wants you to OK it first 'cause it's not exactly the same shade of blue you had before."

Brady thanked Doc again. "I owe you a lot, Doc. What can I do to repay you for all you've done? Can I buy you dinner and a bottle of good scotch whiskey?"

"Fixing my fence would be a good start, you asshole! Do you realize you nearly scared me and the kids half to death when you came crashing in here? Thank God you didn't hit a car driving here like that." Doc grinned and looked over at him to see his reaction. "My daughter is as mad as hell at you for that and upsetting the kids. I told her you survived, but I think she wants to read you the riot act."

Brady chuckled. "She's goin' to ream me a new one? Is that what you're saying?" He'd known Julie a long time and figured she'd make a big deal about the bear attack. She'd always said the cabin was too deep into the forest to be safe.

"Anyway, I was glad to help, and I hope you can come by for dinner the first night she's here to make a peace offering. Then she'll make up and be your loving friend again. Maybe then I can get some peace. And the kids would like to hear all about the bear, so you'll still be a hit with them."

"OK, Doc," he said, "but I want to get up to the cabin as soon as the truck is fixed. Let's drive over to Jimbo's shop, and I'll buy us some good steaks for the grill tonight and maybe that whiskey for our nightcaps." Brady took a sip of beer. "And I'll even fix the fence tomorrow since you're so attached to it, you old cuss." He took a sip of his Bass and wound up draining the bottle.

Doc said, "You're one hell of a pain in the ass for my nearest neighbor on the mountain." They toasted with a clink of their bottles and enjoyed the ambiance of a long-term friendship.

***

Two days later, after enduring Doc's long discourse about his limited fence-building skills, Brady returned to his cabin. He pulled the old Ford up next to the front porch and threw the truck door open. Charlie trampled Brady as he bolted out the door.

The dog then began to scout out his old digs by running back and forth around the cabin, sniffing out all recent history before finally bounding up to the front door, where he stopped and waited for his master to open it. He was a medium-size beast with a mottled gray, longish coat with some curl to it, a real mutt of unknown pedigree. At the shelter they had said he was mostly chocolate Lab, but he had no resemblance to that breed as far as Brady could tell. The huge, upright triangular ears seemed to peg some Norwegian elk hound in his genes, but otherwise he was a complete mystery. All Brady knew for certain was that the hound went through dog chow like an animal twice his size.

Brady noticed a few deep claw slashes on the cabin's carved pine door as he dug in his pocket with his free hand for his keys while balancing a bag of groceries in the other. The claw marks extended across the door two or three times and even cut up the panel above the door.

It was a big bear.

His first thought was that he'd better not let Charlie out at night with this critter hanging around their neck of the forest. Charlie was a great companion, but he didn't have the common sense to stay away from a bear. One swipe of a clawed paw from a grizzly would definitely ruin his day.

He and Doc had discussed the bear a lot over the last two days, and they agreed it had to be a grizzly that had migrated south from his normal range in Wyoming. Reports of elk kills over the last year indicated that a few of the big animals now lived in northern Colorado. But they seemed content in the deep forest and remote mountains away from humans. The bear that attacked Brady was the first to make any significant human contact. This one appeared to have staked out a new territory for himself, and he may believe that Brady was the one intruding on his domain.

Brady put the groceries away, made sure everything in the cabin was shipshape, and gave Charlie his second bowl of Purina for the day. As the dog made loud slurping and crunching sounds to show his appreciation, Brady retreated to the bathroom to run cold water over his painful left elbow.

As he waited for the wash basin to fill, he looked in the mirror over the sink and noted that his beard had really grown in over the last few weeks. He looked a bit like the face on the Mountain Man TV dinners he had just unpacked into the freezer compartment of his fridge. Brown eyes on a tanned, muscular face surrounded by a beard, mustache, and hair all in dark brown certainly gave him a rustic appearance. Perhaps too much so. He didn't want the Grizzly Adams look. He decided he would trim it back before he went down to Doc's for dinner the next night. Maybe Julie would be kind enough to cut his hair for him too. In any case, he hoped she liked the new look.

Next, he and Charlie walked down to the garage to check its condition, Charlie diverting into the mountain stream nearby for a long, lapping drink. The new door that One-Armed Joe had attached was a double-layered pine job that would definitely raise the building's level of security—not fancy but built to last. He noticed that the heavy wind shutters he had placed over the garage windows were still intact, but they had been badly damaged by the bear, who must have returned since the altercation two months ago. He must have remembered the food in the freezer and had come back to get more. That also told

Brady that the bear had recovered from the .45-caliber bullet he had managed to fire into the brute.

Inside the garage was another matter. No one had cleaned it up, even though Doc had put away the remaining food that the bears had strewn about the floor. He had even gotten the freezer to latch closed properly. Brady dug around inside the freezer to evaluate any damage and to verify that some items were unmolested. He packed up the rancid packages the bears had ripped open in their frenzy, swept the garage out, and scrubbed the worst of the dried blood from the floor. He finished with cleanup in less than an hour.

Charlie began barking up a storm up the creek a ways, indicating he had found something smelly and unusual. Brady ran out of the garage and hurried along the creek to find the excited canine. Within a hundred yards, he came across Charlie, who was face-to-face with a coyote that would not yield his ground. One look at Brady was all the coyote needed to get him on his way, looking back twice to be sure they really wanted him gone. Then Brady saw the half-eaten carcass of a young mule deer lying in the woods about twenty-five feet from the stream. Charlie was then sampling the day-old delicacy for himself.

Brady pulled Charlie away and examined the carcass. He quickly saw the signs of a huge paw with three-inch-long claws that had lashed the deer's back and the unmistakable bite pattern of the bear. The bear may have jumped it while it had its head down for a sip of fresh mountain water at the stream. The bear had eaten half the animal and tucked the rest of it up in the weeds for a later meal.

Brady stood up straight, still favoring his left foot, and looked around to see where Charlie was now growling. He was farther up the stream, growling with his tail down, and making woofing sounds to get Brady's attention. He had found fresh bear scat and signs that the bear had pawed the ground up as well. This was bad news. It meant the bear was definitely living in the area, close to the cabin, and probably came here every day for water.

Brady didn't want to share his nook of the forest with such an aggressive neighbor. The bear had probably come into the region this spring, found a nice valley with a creek and plentiful food, even if some of it was in Brady's garage, and had been using the area unchallenged for the last two months. This was the bear's home now. When he realized that Brady was back, he would likely think Brady was invading his new domain. Coexistence was not in a grizzly's rule book, so he would view Brady as someone challenging his authority. There could be only one outcome of such a challenge.

***

"Thanks for coming up to help so fast, Joe," Brady said as he shook Joe's hand. "I really appreciate it."

One-Armed Joe, who in reality had two arms but who had lived with his arm in a sling for three months after an accident, put his toolbox in the back of his Dodge Ram. "Well, you should be good now, Brady." He spit out a stream of brown tobacco juice on Brady's grass. "It looks like a fortress or something out of a Stephen King movie."

Brady surveyed their afternoon's work while Charlie wrestled Joe's black Lab. They had put the winter shutters on the cabin and reinforced them with two-by-sixes for extra strength. Then they had built a triple railing around the front porch and reinforced the two front windows and front door with crossbars of two-by-sixes. Joe had argued that Brady was crazy but admitted there was a remote chance his defenses might just work.

"If you see, Doc, tell him I'll be there tomorrow night as planned," Brady said in parting.

"I'll come by in the morning to see if you and Charlie made it through tonight." Joe laughed and slapped Brady on the back. "I'll bring two body bags just in case there's anything left after the bear gets done with you." He swung into the driver's seat of his truck and started up the big engine. "Take care now."

He threw gravel as he pulled out of the driveway, his dog barking from the bed of the truck.

***

The sun set like an orange flare, signaling the beginning of a long vigil. Brady didn't expect any trouble until after midnight, when the grizzly might come to call. So he set about his usual evening routine, building a fire in the stone fireplace, cooking a simple meal, and feeding Charlie. Charlie finished his dinner in three minutes flat and took up his position on the warm throw rug in front of the fireplace.

Brady took some time to cook one of his favorite meals, venison and veal meatballs in peppercorn sauce over wide egg noodles. He had a bottle of Heineken to go with it and ate at the kitchen table while listening to the sour news on the radio. Then he searched for a station that played old rock and roll favorites and retreated to his favorite chair by the fire, picking up a book he had started. It was a newly published Vince Flynn thriller, even though old Vince had been dead for three years before it was even written.

After an hour, Charlie wagged his tail at the door and whined to Brady that he needed to go outside. Brady checked his watch: 10:30 p.m. He looked outside through the crack in the shutters of the side window and saw the flicker of a half-moon through racing clouds. A storm was coming in, but they still had some light out there, even if the moon was low in the western sky.

Brady went to the front door and flipped on the porch light that he and Joe had supplemented with two new floodlights, one on each corner of the porch to illuminate the area in front of and to both sides of the structure. The lights were dazzling, and he could see out about fifty feet to the edge of the nearest bushes and partway into the meadow. If the bear came on a frontal attack, they would at least see him coming.

Brady checked all around and then opened the door to let Charlie bolt out. The dog shot through the gap in the doorway and jumped off the porch onto his favorite grass at the side of the yard to do his business.

Brady stepped out onto the porch like he usually did and listened to the sounds of the night, all the while scanning the limits of the floods. All quiet. He walked to the heavy-duty railing and observed the moon close on the horizon. *It'll be pitch black out here soon*, he thought. *That's when the bear will come.*

Charlie had just sprung up on the porch when he swiveled his head to look across the meadow. Brady heard it too—the snap of a twig and a rustling of bushes a few hundred yards away. If it was an elk picking its way to the creek, it would likely be to the right by the stream. This was probably not an elk. Brady grabbed Charlie's collar and pulled him through the door, bolting it securely.

"Hey, boy," he said to his excited companion. "Maybe we won't have to wait all night after all, eh?" He rubbed the dog's ears and tried to calm him down so that he could be the ears for both of them. Brady turned the radio off, cut the outside lights, and slid open the two front windows so that they could hear movement outdoors.

Brady built up the fire and turned his chair around to face the front door. He then pulled the blanket off the coffee table in front of him to reveal his small defensive arsenal. On the table he had his pump-action Mossberg 500 shotgun loaded with lethal sabot rounds with extra shells in a box nearby. He also had his Winchester 94 lever-action .30-.30 rifle loaded with wadcutter rounds and spare ammo in a bowl at its side. Finally, when it got right down to it, he lifted his Colt .45 semiauto handgun and tucked it in his belt holster.

The only light in the cabin came from the fireplace and a small reading lamp next to Brady's chair. He picked up his book to read while Charlie lay on the rug by his feet. They both listened to the night breeze as it riffled through the aspen leaves near the meadow. Occasionally, the wind would shift and they would hear the burble of the water from the stream nearby. As the breeze picked up, it caused branches to sway and bushes to rustle almost constantly. The moon had vanished, and they were there alone in their small fortress, an island of light in the dark void of night.

The wind seemed to come and go a bit, sounds rose and fell. It became rhythmic white noise after a while. Brady tried to read, but his eyes grew tired, and the book fell from his lap.

***

Woof! Woof! Grr!

Brady woke when Charlie, now leaning against his knee, began to bark nervously. The wind was striking fiercely outside, causing the curtains on the front windows to flap wildly and bringing in a cacophony of stormy chaos. Rain began to fall.

There was a sudden, terrible wrenching sound at the back of the cabin and then a loud crash. The lights went out!

A great, deep roar came from the rear of the cabin, and loud scraping noises soon followed. The bear was there, growling and pounding on the shutters that protected the bedroom windows. Then there was the sound of boards breaking and glass shattering.

No! Not possible.

Brady felt for the .30-.30 in the dark and scooped up the bowl of extra bullets from the table, pouring them into the left-hand pocket of his vest. He patted Charlie on the head in the dark and said, "OK, boy, stay here." Then he got up and placed new logs on the fire to build it up for light. He tried another light switch; everything was dead, even the LED clock light on the stove.

"OK, boy," he said again to the dog that was right on his heels. "The grizzly got the electrical box somehow. How'd he do that?"

There was pounding at the rear of the cabin and a tearing sound as if a shutter was being ripped off the side of the house. *Oh shit!* Then a crash as a lamp was knocked off the headstand by the bedroom window.

Brady felt his way along the wall of the hallway where he could hear what sounded like a gnawing sound and grumpy guttural *ruffs* as the bear worked on the remains of a shutter or crossbar. He smelled that musky odor again, the bear's smell. He pushed open the bedroom door just as a lightning bolt flashed. In the strobe-like light, Brady saw the bear chewing his way through the two-by-six brace that held the shutter in place. The lower part of the shutter had already been pulled away, and a huge paw reached under the wooden brace. If the bear tore that off, he could climb right into the room.

Without hesitating, Brady raised the Winchester, levered a round into the chamber, and fired right at the shutter where the bear's body should be. He heard the bullet hit the wood with a deafening report. The roar of the rifle and the flash from the muzzle filled the room. He ran to the window for a second shot, but the bear was gone! He could hear it running along the side of the cabin toward the front porch, growling and grunting as he thrashed through the bushes.

Brady racked another round into the firing chamber and turned carefully to retreat back to the living room. He was temporarily blinded by the discharge of his weapon. He walked with a hand on the wall as his eyes adjusted to the darkness again. In the living room, the glow of the rising fire provided an ambient view of the interior. The only images of the outside came from occasional flashes of lightning. Thunder rumbled across the valley, disguising the movements of the bear. Brady's hearing and night vision began to return.

There was a loud crash on the front porch and the rending of wood as the bear ripped off one of the heavy boards that made up the railings. Charlie ran to one of the windows, alternately growling and barking wildly, running forward and then backing away from a fight. Brady raised the rifle and faced the window where Charlie pointed.

A huge crash against the window shook the whole cabin, breaking the glass and splintering the window frame. One of the two-by-sixes seemed to snap with the blow. In the darkness, Brady fired three rapid shots through the window where he thought the bear must be. A roar from outside told him at least one bullet found its mark.

The bear roared again and charged the window. This time, his entire head and one shoulder pushed through the upper half of the window, and the window itself tore out of the frame. The bear struggled to break all the way through but was stopped by other heavy cross braces. He paused there, pushing and squirming to enter the home.

Brady jumped backward and tripped on the coffee table. He fell against his chair and slid off to its left. He landed on his newly reconstructed left elbow, and the pain paralyzed him for a few moments. *I have to shoot! Now!* The bear was right there, within fifteen feet of him, momentarily stuck in the window. It was the shot he had hoped for. From his prone position on the floor, Brady emptied the rest of his rounds into the bear. But the shots were not true. One grazed the bear's head, and one landed right in the meat of his shoulder. Neither was a kill shot. The bear shrieked with pain and pulled out of the window.

Everything was quiet then, except for the wind, rain, and sporadic thunder. *Maybe he had suffered enough*, Brady thought. *Was that it for the night?*

Brady scrambled to his knees, his elbow ablaze with pain, and tried to reload the Winchester. But he had no bullets in his pocket. When he fell, the ammo must have spilled out onto the floor, and in the dim light, he could not find even one bullet.

He crawled to the coffee table and recovered the loaded shotgun. Fighting the pain in his arm, he pumped a sabot into the chamber. He thought he would pass out from the pain.

Charlie began to bark at the window again, but Brady saw nothing. There was a movement outside that he could hear. Then a lightning flash revealed the silhouette of the giant grizzly just outside the front window, standing upright on his hind legs, seven to eight feet tall, forelegs raised like a wrestler ready for a takedown. His evil eyes seemed to bore into Brady's mind with a reddish glow.

The bear lunged forward and crashed through the window, tearing out the frame entirely; only one last two-by-six kept him from falling into the room. He landed with his belly hung up on the last crossbar. He tried to pull himself forward on powerful forepaws, his claws digging into the floorboards. But his hind legs couldn't step over the last crossbar, and he was held in place for a few moments.

Brady forced himself to stand up, and he raised his weapon to fire. He pumped all seven sabots into the bear's head and shoulders, every shot striking home. The bear reared up in pain and surprise, rolling in torment as he bled profusely on the floor. When he turned to the side, his hind legs fell away from the last crossbar, and he was suddenly free.

The hatred in the bear's eyes was palpable. He stared at Brady and growled while Brady watched, dumbfounded. The bear pulled forward, but his hind legs wouldn't cooperate. He could not walk, but his heavy shoulders could still drag him forward on the floor toward his enemy.

Charlie, now emboldened, ran in and bit the bear's ear, the only appendage small enough for him to attack. The bear shrugged the dog off with a single swat of his left paw. Charlie slid across the floor, whining in surprise.

The bear came closer, using his last strength to attack the human intruder in his domain. The bear was now even with the fallen box of shotgun shells, so Brady couldn't reload. All Brady could do was pull out his old, reliable friend, the Colt. With the bear's menacing jaws only three feet away, he unloaded the pistol into the bear's left eye.

Finally, the bear put his head down and stopped moving.

***

Brady pulled up in front of Doc's home the next evening, successfully avoiding the fence and other vehicles. The good doctor came running out to intercept him, taking Brady by the left elbow, causing him to flinch. "Joe said you had it out with that bear. Is it true? Are you all right?"

"Yeah, Doc. I'm fine, but the bear is not." Brady pulled his arm away from Doc's viselike grip. "But let's not talk about it now, with the kids and Julie here, OK?"

"But you got him, right? You got the bear?"

Charlie ran by just then, flinging a triangular, furry object in the air as he played. Doc noticed and asked, "Say, what's he got there?" Doc squinted at the object. "Is that what I think it is?"

Brady looked Doc straight in the eye and said, "Yeah, kinda." He paused to look at his sidekick hound. "But he earned it."

Then Julie and the kids came out of the house to surround the two men. After a few hugs, the excited boys ran off to see what Charlie was chewing on.

At the Forest Queen Hotel

The terrace bar of the Forest Queen Hotel was packed with all sorts of people, tourists up in Crested Butte for the weekend, locals taking a break after work, and the odd assortment of movie people and critics who show up every year for the annual film festival. Somehow they all pressed together to fill every square inch of the hotel bar and terrace after the first day of previews and short film selections.

Hardy Harris sat at one of the patio tables near the river with his floppy-eared basset hound named Old Blue. Hardy sipped a Red IPA from the local brewhouse to help him cool off on the warm summer evening. Blue slept under the steel mesh table and dreamed of jack rabbits. They had come to the butte to enjoy the celebratory atmosphere of the festival and to listen to an old friend play guitar.

As Hardy enjoyed the music, four men walked past the guitar player to a round outdoor table made of steel mesh at the edge of the hotel patio and sat on the steel chairs that surrounded it. They were brusque and seemed to be irritated before they even sat down. The musician called over to them to be careful next to the railing, since it was not very sturdy and the mountains had just received a big rain earlier that day, swelling the normally shallow Coal Creek behind them into a raging torrent. Maybe they ignored him, or maybe they just didn't hear.

The man who seemed to be in charge, the heavyset one with a suspiciously full head of brown hair and a mustache, took the seat facing the musician and waved over the server. The taller, rugged, dark-haired guy wearing a leather jacket and wrangler boots sat facing the river that flowed rapidly just beside the edge of the terrace. He seemed on edge, perhaps angry about something they had been discussing. The older gentleman in the gray suit took the seat opposite the man in charge. He ordered a margarita when the waiter came to the table. The fourth man, the only one wearing a Hawaiian shirt, short pants, and Crocs shoes was left with the chair on the river side of the table so that he backed onto the low, black metal fence that separated the terrace from the torrent behind him. The last to order, he asked for a glass of chardonnay and opened his compact laptop computer on his knee as the others talked. He shuffled his chair as far forward as he could, noticing the loose tiles beneath him. The server gave them all menus.

The mustached man, named Bob, went around the table to see if anyone wanted to order anything else. "OK, so we've got about half an hour till our reservation at the restaurant, so we can have a drink. Does anyone want an appetizer? They've got crab cakes. Or maybe the calamari?" He turned to Bernie with the computer. "Hey, Bernie. What's the name of this place again, the fancy restaurant?"

"The Gourmet Noodle. It's some new place I heard about at the lobby bar last night. Supposed to be the koolio place to be. The bartender said all the local celebs go there."

"So it's close by, right?" Bob turned away to see what had happened to the waiter.

Bernie called up Siri on his iPhone to get directions to the GN. Siri was not cooperating, so he tried Google Maps next but with no results. He shifted his chair, and it tipped sideways a few degrees, bumping into the fence, the tiles shifting under him. He looked across the terrace to see that the whole deck seemed to be a sea of undulating tiles, some loose, some simply tipping up at odd angles. Bernie thought, *Cousin Jake could make a killing here on the slip and fall lawsuits alone!*

The waiter came with the drinks and passed them out in rotation, thinking all the time: *Bourbon for the fat cat, chardonnay for short pants, margarita for the suit, and Fat Tire for the Marlboro Man.* He took Bob's order for calamari and crab cakes and disappeared into the side door of the hotel, tripping on the loose step at the entrance.

Bob took a sip of his whiskey and resumed the conversation they had started on the walk to the hotel. "OK. So the two clips we screened as a teaser didn't go so well. Maybe we need to tweak them a bit or try other scenes."

Bernie looked up from the screen and commented, "I didn't think the clips were the best choice for the screening anyway. They were too short to give a feel for the characters."

The Marlboro Man said, "And they weren't even in my book anyway. They were just filler you idiots added later, for Christ's sake. They had nothing to do with the story."

Barry, the producer and the oldest of the group, griped, "It's all because of Zubelovski! That moron liked the shot because it shows Vana's cleavage in a close-up, and the second shot was his girlfriend's idea. We should never have listened to him." Barry Levinstien was not a man to let business interfere with the quality of his production. He told himself, *Never go into business with the Russian mob.*

"Well," Bob quipped, "we may have to have some of his input, but we can minimize his ideas. Maybe we can get his people off the studio grounds once in a while." He stared at Barry and downed the rest of his bourbon, ordering a double as the waiter went by.

Barry looked at the youngish women at the nearest table, who seemed to know they were movie people. "Look." He leaned forward so as to be heard over the music and the din of conversations, the street noise, and the roar of the river. "I told Zubelovski that he would be a silent partner from the beginning, but he's just worked his way into things. He wouldn't take no for an answer." He rolled his eyes. "And that gutter whore he calls his girlfriend *thinks* she can act. I caught her in the costume trailer one day, trying on burlesque outfits. She's very pushy." He looked over at Bernie. "Ask Bernie. She's been trying to talk him into writing a part for her."

Bernie looked up from the screen again, still no location for the Gourmet Noodle found, and remembered the way Vana had sat on his lap one day in his trailer as he typed in dialogue. She could be very persuasive, and before he knew what happened, he had added her into a barroom scene wearing the revealing burlesque rags she'd had on that day and in today's preview. While he enjoyed her intimate attention, he felt used and cheapened by the incident. He thought he should have taken the gig with Woody Allen to work on the new *Brighton Beach* script instead of this debacle of a movie.

"She told me you wanted her in a scene, Barry. I thought you were just trying to keep Mr. Z happy." Bernie gulped nearly all his wine in one go and waved the empty glass at a waitress, who noticed and smiled at him. "Now Vana seems to think she's the star of the movie and is acting the part all the time. Her English is pretty bad."

"She's trying to reincarnate Greta Garbo with a Gorky accent. And she wears that awful Gypsy Rose Lee outfit everywhere to be recognized." Marlboro Man laughed. "I saw her wearing it at the screening just now. She came up to me afterward, said 'Mickey, dahling,' and gave me such a big kiss. That got Zubelovski irritated."

Bob took the lead again. "OK, OK. So let's get down to it before Z shows up for dinner. Plan B, Barry. We rewrote the entire script and can chuck the old stuff. Randy here is on board with the rewrite, isn't that right, Randy?"

Randal Bang, a.k.a. the Marlboro Man, author of the popular romantic Western *Gone to Hell for Tara*, sighed and agreed. "Well, we had to do something with that turd of a script your first writer, James, came up with. Why didn't you check that shit before he got so far? Anyway, Bernie had some great ideas and returned to the story I wrote. I think it reads much better now—the screenplay, I mean."

Bernie thought about his last month of furious writing to try to save this dog of a project for Barry Levinstien Productions. It wasn't the first time Barry had begged Bernie to "tweak" some piece of steaming horseshit. Bernie wished he had taken the other job. Woody was cheap, but he made classy movies. "I finished the revisions last night and have it all right here on my laptop, the only copy in existence so that Z can't get his hands on it."

Bob commented, "Bernie did a marvelous job, Barry. We can go over it later—you know, after dinner, when Zubelovski and Vana leave."

Then from the street, a woman called out, "Oh, Mickey! Hello!" They all looked toward the street to see Vana smiling widely, waving her long, uncovered arm at them. Zubelovski was with her and another man who was wearing a long black leather coat in the late-summer heat—the bodyguard. They marched into the hotel and came out the terrace door, headed their way.

"Oh shit!" Bernie looked for a way to duck out the rear of the patio, but it was too late for that. He would have to put up with another evening with Vana pawing his leg as he tried not to let Mr. Z see what she was doing. She was totally indiscreet in those situations. He tried to stand up but was trapped by the arms of the unyielding chair that had gotten tangled in the low railing behind him. He closed the computer and hid it next to him on the chair at the last minute.

Vana burst out the side door of the hotel and onto the patio, a platinum blonde dressed in the very tight-fitting scarlet gown she had worn all day, her cleavage on the verge of spilling out of a low-cut neckline trimmed in sequins, its kind not worn in public perhaps since the screening of *Gone with the Wind*. Z followed right behind her with his guard in tow.

Vana stopped on the last step down to the terrace to give the other customers a chance to appreciate her gown with the slit up to her hip on the right side, posing like Angelina did at the last Oscars. Several people applauded as she dazzled them with her smile and a flash of skin. The men at the table rose to receive her, and she stepped off the stair in the direction of their table, her hand held before her in midair so that Mickey could accept it and kiss its back, as would a true gentleman.

Somehow, on her way from the stair, her high heel caught on the uneven tile of the terrace, and she lost her balance, lurching forward in an unladylike rush as she tried to remain upright. She stumbled right into Mickey, who was thrown back against the table in the tight quarters of the terrace. He in turn banged into the table, as he tried to maintain his balance while holding on to the body of the young woman who now looked up into his eyes gratefully. That was when her cleavage popped free of all constraints.

The table jolted backward, knocking the others to their seats or sending them into each other for support. Bernie was pushed right back against the railing, clutching at anything he could reach, finding only his laptop to hold on to. Over the railing he went, in the dark of the night, and into the rushing waters of Coal Creek. He vanished downstream in a flash, bobbing to the surface of the rapids only once, holding the computer out of the water, as if in that act he could be saved.

The commotion woke the somnolent Old Blue, who rolled upright and barked out his surprised commentary. *Baroo!*

It took a minute for Bernie's tablemates to realize what had happened, as Vana straightened her dress to cover the double wardrobe malfunction that had caught everyone's attention and was recorded on an iPhone camera by one enterprising teenager who was there with his family.

Only Hardy saw Bernie go over the railing and into the water. He called 911 and ran down the side of the river where he could find a path. Old Blue trotted steadily behind, careful not to slip into the turbulent creek. He had a fear of water and hated paddling in cold streams.

***

Bernie was washed downstream and was not rescued that night. His body was found by divers the next day, floating in the reservoir outside of town. His death made the front-page news of the local paper and held a minute of the TV news for only one night. But Vana was interviewed by several reporters who insisted she wear the same dress she had on that evening, and she willingly obliged. The YouTube video of the wardrobe incident went viral overnight and became the talk of Hollywood and the media, with forty million hits the first day. Bernie's soggy computer was recovered but useless. A copy of the final revised script was found on the Microsoft Cloud, since it was typed in the new Word 10, which saves a copy of everything you write, whether you want it to or not. Zubelovski's nephew, an adept computer hacker, located it by employing software only he knew how to use.

***

The movie *Gone to Hell for Tara* opened to rave reviews a year later, starring the newly signed sensation, Vana Z, a surprising discovery of the fabled Barry Levinstien Studios. The film did so well at the box office that Zubelovski commissioned Randal Bang to write two more sequels to his novel, both best sellers, with a built-in movie deal for them as well. Everyone was happy and thrilled with the success of the films. They all made a lot of money.

Even Bernie became an unwitting star as the author of the original revised screenplay and contributor in absentia for the sequels. He received three Oscar nominations, one win, and a star on Hollywood Boulevard.

A Night in Old Durango

Zach Thorne felt really calm after a long night of carousing with his buddies from the unofficial rugby team. They had hit a couple of their favorite bars and consumed way too much beer. That was why Zach was riding the drunken bus, the free, friendly town transport for those too dangerously inebriated to drive themselves home. He figured that he would be an easy target for the town Mounties if he drove himself.

The bus bounced along the highway just inside the Durango city limits to Zach's apartment building, where the rents were low enough for a student to get by. At least he could share it with his roommate, Sarah, a very patient woman who suffered through some of his more negligent episodes of drinking and lethargy as long as he made his rent contribution.

The old codger driving the drunken bus tonight was Hardy, a retired marine who volunteered his time one night a week. He was a good sort who knew Zach pretty well after chauffeuring him home in a confused state more than once. Hardy said that he had often tied one on in his younger days, and he could understand the need some people had for their excesses. Besides, he brought his friendly basset hound, Old Blue, with him, and the dog seemed to relate to the drunks better than most people. Blue lay on the seat close to Hardy, where he could look out the front window and greet new riders as they staggered up the steps of the free bus.

They approached the somewhat seedy Durango Estates East, three brown, wood-sided buildings pushed into the edge of the national forest close to a minor trailhead. Hardy slowed his vehicle to pull into the gravel parking lot of Zach's humble abode when something unexpected happened.

A man dressed in short pants and a plaid wool shirt ran right in front of the bus, causing Hardy to slam on the brakes and Old Blue to sit up and bark in surprise. *Baroo!* The man appeared familiar to both Zach and Hardy, a wild look in the whites of his eyes as he stopped in front of the bus, arms waving over his head, a machete flashing in one hand, shouting inaudible obscenities before bolting across the highway and into the trees.

"Oh shit! It's Harry!" Zach recognized his rugby buddy in the instant the headlights held him. "Oh shit! Oh damn!"

Old Blue commented again as Zach slumped down the stairs, thanked Hardy, and stepped into the freshly fallen inches of snow. *Now what?* he thought as Hardy turned the bus around and its headlights swept the trees where his errant mate had vanished. He'd have to go look for Harry in a minute. Right now, Zach's mind was focused on where Harry appeared to be fleeing from, which was apartment 2B, Zach's home.

Zach took a few deep breaths of crisp air to try to snap out of the haze that he had successfully constructed over the long evening. The snow had stopped falling, and the full moon peeked out of the gray clouds. *That explains a few things*, he thought. Harry's more outrageous moments tracked with the lunar cycle.

Zach skidded across the snowy lot to the stairs that led to 2B. Before he could insert the right key into the lock, he heard Sarah shout, "Stay out of here, you lunatic! I called the cops!"

"It's me, Sarah! Don't shoot!"

The door opened, and sure enough, Sarah stood there holding the .38 Special her father had given her for self-defense. "Come in and close the door. That crazy friend of yours was just here, and I ain't letting him in again."

Zach got the download. "When I got home, Harry was already in here. Came in through my bedroom window and was waving that damn big knife of yours around like a manic!" Her eyes were wide with fear as she spit out his name. Her otherwise friendly features were tight and her face red. "What the hell is the matter with him now? I told him to get out, but he locked himself in the bathroom and said he'd kill himself right there."

"I'm sorry. It's the full moon again. I think . . . hell, I don't know!"

"Well, I can't take it anymore. I called the cops. If he comes back, I'll shoot the son of a gun."

Zach ran outside and across the road. "Harry! Where the hell are you? What are you doing, scaring Sarah like that? You dumb . . ."

Then he walked to the other side of the road to shout behind the apartment building in case Harry backtracked that way. Yelling into the darkness produced no result. Harry was either long gone or he was hiding. It really pissed Zach off. He pounded the fence that surrounded the dumpsters with his fist as he walked past, knocking a board loose. "Great! What's next?"

He slogged back through a couple of snowdrifts to the parking lot, where two city patrol cars were now parked, bubble lights flashing blue and red over the whole complex. Two officers were at the door of 2B, one with his gun drawn, as they talked to Sarah, who still had her pistol in hand. She was talking a blue streak and was getting a sympathetic response from the cops. Two more cruisers pulled into the lot with their lights flashing. Two county Mounties emerged from the cars and called up to their brothers standing in front of 2B.

Then Sarah saw Zach and pointed at him with her free hand, causing all the cops to turn his way and give him the evil eye. *What the hell?* he thought. *What'd I do?* He stepped into the parking lot and was beset by the deputies, one of whom had his hand on his holster. The other talked into the microphone on his lapel.

"Are you Mr. Thorne?"

"Yes, I'm Zach Thorne. My friend is the guy you're after."

"Oh yeah? Let's see an ID."

Zach reached for his wallet but found an empty pocket at the back of his cargo pants. *Oh shit!* He'd lost his damn wallet!

Then one of the town cops said, "Zachary R. Thorne? Hey, we have you listed on an outstanding bench warrant." He looked at the deputies. "Seems you didn't show up in court for Judge Brennan." He pulled out his set of handcuffs.

Holy shit! Zach's sluggish mind processed that this evening wasn't going the way he had planned. He should have made it to court that day, but it had slipped his mind. *So what? Is that a crime?* It was set at 9:00 a.m. anyway, an outrageously early time to do anything.

The cop approached with his cuffs to hook him up. Zach panicked. His addled brain wasn't up to this. His fight-or-flight reflex was all screwed up. With animal instinct he pushed the cop back. He needed time to think. Thinking was hard right now. *Where was Harry anyway? That menace!*

The cops had all gone on alert at the pushing action. The deputy standing next to him grabbed Zach's left arm. Zach shrugged it off like the guy was a beginner in a scrum line. Zach was a big guy; no ordinary rugby player could hold on to him for long. He felt good about this. Maybe he could talk them out of hauling him in. Sometimes cops were reasonable.

Then both deputies grabbed him like a piece of meat and held him in place while the guy with the cuffs clipped one wrist. Zach went into panic mode. He pulled his right arm free and clocked the city cop in the face. The deputy lost his footing and went down, cursing Zach. Zach struggled valiantly but was thrown to the ground while he continued to punch and kick the four cops who tried to subdue him. He landed a couple of blows with his foot and a fist before a black shadow suddenly shut his vision down.

***

Zach dreamed he was inside a washing machine on the wash cycle, beaten by unseen baffles on all sides. One eye didn't focus right for a few seconds and he felt sick. Then he puked all over the bench he was on. Beer and blood flowed everywhere. He managed to sit up, but his head felt like it would explode at any moment. He ran his left hand over his face and thought something was wrong. Some of his otherwise striking features felt swollen and out of place. Everything hurt when he touched it.

He stood up with difficulty, slipping in the puddle of puke on the floor. He was surrounded by iron bars on two sides of the little room. Concrete block walls completed the enclosure. He shifted over to another bench and sat down. He held his head in both hands for a while, trying to remember what had happened. *Oh shit! I slugged a cop!*

He looked around. White walls and gray bars signaled that he was in the Durango jail. He had punched a town cop, so that's why he was here and not at the county lockup. Well, at least he knew where he was, having been here before. Not so bad. He'd have to call Mark, who was treasurer of the rugby club. He could bail him out with the rugby fund, the special account that they all contributed to for jailhouse disasters.

Zach reached for his phone. Nothing! *Huh? The cops must have taken it. Oh shit! Or did I leave that at the bar too?* Without it, he didn't have any of the club phone numbers. This was a really shitty evening!

Zach started calling out to get someone's attention. He was in this cell by himself, and the cages around him were all empty, which was unusual for a Friday night. No one answered or came to see what he wanted. They either couldn't hear him or they didn't care to come in to talk.

Then Zach noticed a camera set just outside his cell, hanging from the ceiling. It was watching him. It made him nervous. Why were they watching him but not responding? *Motherhumpers!* He got up on the bench, reached out to the camera, and got a hand on it.

***

Officer Bruce Johansen had just come on duty at 2:00 a.m. and was making the rounds in the drunk tank and the other usual areas. He stayed out of cellblock B as he was told. They had thrown some whacko in there to settle down, and he was to monitor him remotely while doing his other duties. It was a quiet night so far.

Johansen stepped into the restroom to straighten the few hairs on his bald head and inspect his thin, wan features for a moment. Then he returned to his desk with a cup of coffee and switched his computer to the camera viewing software. He pulled up the camera in cellblock B and then promptly spilled the brew all over his keyboard.

He saw a misshapen face right up in the fisheye lens of the camera and a huge fist punching the machine over and over. The image on his screen rocked back and forth with each blow, breaking up every once in a while as the sideways motion increased. The prisoner stopped punching for a moment, and the face came closer to the lens, lips moving perversely. Then more punches.

Johansen found it surreal to see all this fury in the black-and-white monitor, silent like an old movie, so he moved the sound widget up to hear what the man was saying and immediately regretted it. "Fricking cops. Blazing assholes, think they can watch me . . . damn fu . . ." There was loud banging on the camera at the same time. He switched the sound off again and panicked. This was supposed to be the quiet sleepover shift. Now it had all gone to hell.

**

"OK! Is everyone ready? We lost visual on cellblock B, so we have to assume we have a man or men loose in there, out of containment of any kind. So we go into an unknown situation." Sergeant Lanny York had come into the station to take control of the bizarre situation on the chief's direct order. He had assembled a breach team of seven men. Johansen was the lead man in, carrying a riot shield on his left arm and sporting a fully charged Taser in his right hand. He was assigned to use the shield to deflect projectiles and, if possible, pin the prisoner against the wall with it. Then he would stick the assailant with all fifty thousand volts, and the two columns of men, three deep, would wrestle the felon to the floor and beat the crap out of him before applying restraints. They were counting on Johansen as point man. As a thin, wiry type, he didn't look like much, and some of the men weren't sure about him, but his file pegged him as the guy for the job.

York would monitor the action from the rear with a shotgun loaded with alternating beanbags and rubber slug rounds in case they were overrun. *Piece of cake*, York thought. This method worked every time back in '09 during the state prison riot. Only five cops were injured and two prisoners killed. Acceptable losses then and now. If all went well, York might get a promotion. He ran his hand through his thinning hair and then twisted his waxed mustache as he smiled to himself.

***

Zach was sitting on the bench when the steel door to cellblock B slammed open, the doorknob drilling a hole into the plaster wall beside it. A package of men rushed through the doorway, all dressed in black riot gear and shouting at the top of their lungs: "Go! Go! Go!" After they entered the room, they formed a flying wedge with a tall, skinny, frightened-looking guy at its apex, holding a clear plastic riot shield and flashing a Taser in his right hand. They seemed confused when they found the main corridor empty and only one man in the whole cellblock. Then they focused on the camera dangling from the ceiling, and they repositioned in front of Zach's cell.

A heavyset man with a receding hairline cautiously entered the corridor, holding a shotgun at the ready. He looked like he was enjoying himself until he realized Zach was staring at him. Then he stiffened up and ordered the men to prepare for a final breach.

One of the officers inched gingerly forward and put a key in the lock on Zach's cell door, then retreated to the rear of the wedge. Next, Johansen, still holding the Taser and shield, reached out to unlock the door. He seemed terrified.

Zach made eye contact like he would in any rugby match and gave Johansen a look that told him he was going down. That caused Johansen to drop the Taser as Zach studied the wedge of seven men facing him. They had problems. First, the door to the cell was too narrow for two men to cross through side by side, so their formation would fall apart as they entered. Second, in a scrum every man locked arms with the others, with a big, tough son of a gun in the lead, someone who wouldn't go down. The rest of the men forced him forward in the formation. The wedge relied on their combined power to push their opponents back.

These guys would come through the door one at a time. And the tip of the spear looked like he was about to lose his lunch.

The cop with the shotgun shouted, "Breach! Breach!"

The others yelled, "Go! Go! Go!," and the door was unlocked.

Problem. The door opened outward.

Zach was outraged. He shouted, "Bring it on, you assholes! Bring it on!"

***

Police Chief Duane Parker was beside himself at 6:00 a.m. when he finally got things straightened out at the station. It was the worst clusterfuck he had seen in his twenty-eight years in law enforcement. He blamed Sergeant York for this mess and would deal with him appropriately when he had the names of all the dumbasses involved.

He had arrived earlier to find that York's breach plan had failed in the most spectacular fashion possible. On entering the cell of one dazed drunk, the lead man, Johansen, had tripped and dropped the Taser. The others who followed were bowled aside by a man who was in fear for his life and in Incredible Hulk mode as he defended himself. Johansen had broken his wrist in the altercation that followed. Two men had been tased, and another had broken his hand against the concrete wall in the fight. As far as he could tell, his men managed to tase each other, missing the prisoner entirely.

In the excitement, York had fired his weapon in an unauthorized manner, hitting the prisoner once with a beanbag, shooting Officer Gomez in the ass with a rubber slug intended for bear control, not human use, and wounding his colleagues with inaccurate fire. He even managed to hit himself in the cheek with one of the ricocheting slugs that were not intended for use in confined spaces. Now Gomez and York were in the hospital with gunshot wounds, Officer Jerkin was in the cardiac ward suffering from arrhythmia from being tased, and two others had been released after treatment.

The chief stood in front of the cell in block B where the prisoner lay on his side on the floor, handcuffed and with his arms behind his back, his ankles shackled, and his feet pulled up behind him and cuffed to his hands in a dangerous hog-tie position. A pool of vomit covered the floor, with the prisoner's face smeared in the center of it.

This fiasco might force him to resign. He put his hands over his face and swore to himself. *What a screwup!* At least there was no video of the whole affair and no photos to leak out. Parker was grateful for small favors. He could thank the prisoner for the lack of video.

He called his only uninjured officer into the cellblock to enter the prisoner's cell and get him out of the hog-tie position. Thank God he was still alive after a night like that. He had the semiconscious prisoner recuffed, with his hands in front of him, after which Parker evaluated his state of health for himself. Then they removed the cuffs entirely and left the prisoner on the bench to sleep.

Earlier, Zach had been taken to the hospital with the injured officers and was said to be sleeping off a heavy binge enhanced by tasing and a beating. If the injured prisoner had any trace of a concussion, the whole police department could expect a lawsuit.

Chief Parker walked calmly to his office and called the city attorney, Hank Warner, at his home to discuss options. His men, led by Sergeant York, wanted to charge the drunk with numerous offenses ranging from assaulting an officer to resisting arrest, all based on the initial warrant. On top of that, they wanted to add about eleven charges that resulted from the man defending himself against a massed police action, which any good attorney would simply turn into a colossal police brutality case. He hoped Warner had some creative ideas to avoid going to court.

***

The prisoner slumped in his chair opposite Chief Parker and the city attorney in the interrogation room. He didn't look too crisp with a bruised face, his left eye swollen completely shut, a split lip, and black stitches here and there from the hospital visit. He had both hands bandaged like a boxer wearing white mitts, and his arm was in a sling; the doctor had noted in his report that the injury appeared to be the result of stomping. Parker would have to talk to his boys about the use of excessive force when a prisoner is already in custody. It just made the department look bad.

Warner started out with the approach they had agreed on, which was to play hardball and hope the prisoner would be cowed into taking a deal. "Mr. Zachary R. Thorne, you've had quite a night. We're going to charge you with sixteen serious felonies. You engaged in a significant crime spree, my friend, but you are going down hard this time." When the prisoner didn't respond, Warner leaned forward. "Can you hear me, boy?"

Before either Parker or Warner could say another word, the door of the room jerked open and the chief's secretary, Melody, reached in to hand him a smartphone. "It's all over the internet—with photos."

On the phone's screen was a well-lighted, full-color photograph of the hog-tied prisoner lying on the floor of the hospital emergency room last night. *Holy shit!* Melody wordlessly indicated that he should thumb to the next picture. He did so and found a close-up image of an unconscious Zach Thorne with blood all over his heavily bruised face. He thought again, *Oh shit! We're screwed!*

The chief passed the phone to Warner and wondered to himself what happened to cops who spent time at the state prison in Florence. Warner's eyebrows nearly shot off his forehead when he looked at the photos.

The prisoner chose that moment to raise his head and mutter, "My uncle's an attorney."

***

A week later Old Blue woofed in recognition as a familiar passenger climbed on board with his one good arm. Hardy

squinted and said, "Jeez, Zach! It must have been quite a party."
Hardy had heard reports of what had happened at the jail.

Zach dropped onto a seat near the front of the bus. "Yeah, it's
a long story, but I won. All charges were dropped, and every
member of the rugby club had their traffic tickets rescinded."

"The story I heard seemed a little over the top. Something
about *bring it on?*" He gave Zach a sideways glance as the corner
of his mouth curled upward in a grin.

"Yeah, I guess." Zach tried to smile.

He was headed home early tonight, playing it safe in a town
where the Mounties were waiting for any excuse for a grudge
match. The last thing he wanted was a repeat of last Friday
night's activities. Things were looking up now that he had a little
money coming his way from the town council. They called it a
stipend. *Yes, sir. It was a pleasant night.*

Hardy angled the drunken bus into Zach's parking lot.
Something darted past the bus on the left side as Zach stood up
to disembark.

Hardy gave Zach a sheepish grin and asked, "Say, wasn't that
your wacky buddy headed for the woods?"

Zach sat down again. "Hardy, can I just ride back into town
again? I'm not sure I'm ready to go home just yet."

The Rifle Stickup

Jeff Hollings had just finished work at the City Market gas station that Friday night when his buddy Rich pulled up next to his rusty Ford pickup truck.

"Hey, I got us a deluxe Tombstone pizza, one of my favorites," he called out from the cab of his Toyota. "You ready to roll yet?"

"Yeah, just punched out. Follow me."

Jeff and Rich planned to watch a DVD of the newer version of *Guardians of the Galaxy* at his home while eating home-cooked pizza. Home baked, but not homemade. Rich had already picked up the frozen pie. They caravanned over to the local liquor store, the Plaza, and parked near the glass front windows next to a late-model black Charger that had seen better days.

"How about a twelve-pack of Avery IPA? That should do us for the night," Jeff said.

"Yeah, sounds good. I'll grab a pint of Tin Cup too," Rich said as they both charged the door of the shop. Rich entered first and snickered as he cut Jeff off, then headed for the whiskey aisle while Jeff turned for the beer cooler at the back of the store.

Rich reached the cornucopia of malted wonder and scanned the shelf for Tin Cup, searching for a pint bottle of the same. No luck. *They must keep them up front behind the register,* he thought. He walked quickly back to the checkout area as Jeff set the twelve-pack down on the counter. They both reached for their wallets at the same time.

"Hi, Julie. How's it going?" Jeff asked charmingly, knowing his old high school girlfriend was now dating Earl Hudson, a local realtor and man about town. Earl was a couple of years older than Jeff and was successful by local standards. They had been competitors for Julie's attention in high school a few years back. Jeff was still trying to get his feet on the ground for what he knew would be a stellar career in something, whenever he figured out what that would be.

Julie had a distant look in her eye and seemed nervous behind her cloth face mask, unlike her usual friendly self. *Jeez*, thought Jeff. *I hope she doesn't have the COVID. She looks kind of pale.* Remembering that he had forgotten to put on a mask at the door, he dug in his pocket for the rumpled surgical one he carried for such occasions. Maybe the fact that he'd forgotten his face covering made her tense.

"Sorry about that. I forget all the time." He looked her in the eye again and realized there was something wrong. She didn't move, just stood as still as a post while her eyes darted sideways in an edgy way. He couldn't see what she was looking at because of the way the new plexiglass window was positioned on the counter. Another COVID-19 requirement in these days of extra caution.

"Hey," Rich said when he noticed her body language. "What's the matter, Jules? You look like—"

They both jumped back when a man with a shotgun stood up and focused his attention on them across the counter. All Jeff saw at first was the 12 gauge at close range. That told him why Julie was practically catatonic. He raised his hands in front of him to ward off the danger.

"Jesus Christ! It's a damn stickup!" Rich shouted frantically. "Hell, Jeff. Do something!"

The man with the shotgun pointed the barrel at Rich and shouted, "Don't do a goddamned thing or I'll blow your face off."

Julie's eyed widened as she looked behind Jeff. He realized they were surrounded when a gun barrel pressed into the back of his neck.

"Don't even think about it," a second man said with force behind Jeff's head, alcohol breath and all. "Either of you packin'?"

The man frisked Jeff first, then Rich, as they both held their hands up, shaking.

"Take it easy, man," Rich said, trying to ward off any trouble. "We're just here for booze. That's all."

"You OK, Julie?" Jeff asked, concern in his voice. "They hurt you?"

"Shut up, dumbass!" shouted the man, who now clubbed Jeff on the back of his neck. "No talkin'."

Jeff fell forward against the counter and dropped to his knees as stars shot through his vison. Rich reached over to stabilize him so that he wouldn't fall to the floor. The man whacked Rich on his shoulder with the revolver a couple of times to stop him from helping his friend.

"That goes for you too, asshole." The man pushed him forward into the counter and forced him onto his knees next to Jeff, who was clinging to the countertop.

"Jeff," Julie called out. "Are you OK?"

The man behind the counter reached over with the butt of the shotgun and slammed it into the side of her head. She staggered and held on to the register for support.

"Shut up, bitch. Now open the register for me, or I'll hit you again."

Julie looked terrified but complied by opening the till. The guy with the shotgun pushed her aside and started pulling out wads of cash from the drawer. He stuffed it into a cloth bag that he held in his other hand. He looked carefully at the cash and grabbed Julie by her long hair.

"Where's the rest of it, bitch?" he snarled. "We were told you'd have a couple of thousand on a Friday night." He shook her violently. "Where's the rest of it?"

"That's all we have in the till. The rest gets put into the safe every hour." She whimpered. "I put it in the floor safe as we go along."

"Get it out of there." He looked down and saw the opening to a steel box built into the floor next to him. He pushed her to the floor so quickly that she almost fell on her face, barely catching herself on her hands and knees. "Hurry up, bitch."

"But I can't!" Julie cried loudly. "I don't know how. It just goes in there until the boss comes by tomorrow. He has the key." She began to sob into her hands.

"What the hell?" The man looked up at the other. "Damn it, Wiley. Why didn't you know about this? You were supposed to find out everything about this dump."

Wiley stepped up to the plexiglass and frowned. "That asshole Bruce didn't say nothing about a safe." He was sweating profusely and wiped his face with the back of his hand. "Shit. I don't know. Can we pull it out of the floor? We could work on it later."

"No, you dipshit. This looks like it's built in. Probably set in cement." Mr. Shotgun swore a blue streak and then pounded the butt of his weapon on the shelving behind him, breaking a dozen bottles of bourbon as the shelf collapsed. "We don't have time to work on it. We're already over our time limit. Let's get out of here."

"What do we do with these guys, Hank? Shoot 'em? They can ID us."

"So can she, you dummy," Hank said. "I don't want to get in any deeper than we already are." His eyes were wild as he looked desperately around. Spotting the door to the storeroom, he motioned toward it with the 12 gauge. "In there. We'll tie them up."

Hank grabbed Julie by the arm and muscled her onto her feet. Then he propelled her along the counter to the rear of the store. Wiley pushed the two customers in the same direction.

"You guys behave, or I'll kill your little friend here," Hank said. "Now get in there and get down on your knees."

Once inside the storeroom, Wiley used packing cord that was lying on a stack of boxes to tie Jeff's hands behind his back and his ankles together. He tied him to a post in the middle of the room, then did the same to Rich. Finally, he placed packing tape across their mouths so that they couldn't call out. Next, he tied Julie's hands behind her back and taped her mouth shut. He began to tie her ankles together, but before he could finish, they all heard a voice from the front of the store.

"Anybody here?" someone called out. "Are you open?"

"It must be a customer, Wiley. We're taking too long." They hesitated long enough to hear the customer help himself to something from the big coolers before the front door bell clanked a few times. Then it was silent again.

"Whoever it was is gone." Hank eyed a door at the back of the storeroom. "Out there," he whispered. "Let's go out the back way and then around to the car. We'll take her with us for insurance."

In a minute the men had forced a kicking and muttering Julie out the door. Hank grabbed her by the throat and squeezed until she gave in and staggered forward. Jeff listened as they clumped around the back of the building on the loose gravel. After a short time, they heard the throaty roar of the Charger as they pulled out of the parking lot and onto the road.

"Sounds like they're headed north," Rich said through the tape that covered his mouth as he struggled with the cords on his wrists. "That guy really tied these knots tight. My hands feel numb already."

"We have to go after them," Jeff mumbled as he tested the cord that bound his wrists. "See if you can reach my boot knife if I lift my foot up toward you. Then we can cut these ropes and chase those thugs."

Jeff raised his right boot up close to Rich's hands so that he could grab the knife. On the third attempt, Rich took the knife in his fingers and began to delicately slice away at his constraints. After ten minutes of trying to turn the knife around and not stab an arm, he finally cut through the cords on his right wrist. When free, he slashed Jeff's ropes too.

"We'd better get a move on if we're going to catch those guys and get Julie back," Jeff said quietly.

The two men ran out the back door of the liquor store and around the building to their vehicles. Jeff shouted, "I'll call 911. Do you have a handgun in the truck?"

"Yeah, I'll get it. We'll have to take your truck. Mine's about out of go juice." Rich ran to his truck and pulled his Smith & Wesson semiautomatic out of the glove box. Then he raced over to climb into Jeff's old Ford. In a few minutes, they were heading up Highway 13 after the Dodge Charger.

The highway ran north through the outskirts of Rifle and along the side of Government Creek. They drove past the turnoff to Rifle Gap and the reservoir there. The road angled north and then northwest as they encountered the flank of the Grand Hogback, a long, continuous mountain that runs from the Colorado River all the way north for fifty miles to the town of Meeker, Colorado. It was a major barrier to traffic and defined the east margin of Highway 13 as it ran north. It formed the east side of the long Government Creek valley that was also bounded on the west side by the huge mesa called the Roan Plateau. Once in the valley, there were few ways to climb up out of it going either west or east due to the rugged terrain.

There were few cars on the road, so Jeff sped along as fast as his truck could go, trying to catch up to the Charger and the kidnappers. He hoped they would not be driving at their highest possible speed because his Ford could not match the top end of the Charger. But if the men assumed that Jeff and Rich were still tied up, maybe they would be cruising along at a more reasonable speed, trying not to attract attention. Like maybe sixty or seventy miles an hour to match the way most people drove out in the country.

Jeff's cell phone beeped, and he answered the call by driving with one hand and keeping his speed manageable at about eighty-five. The road was straight enough, and he was familiar with it.

"Hello, Chief Walters," he greeted the town police chief. "We're headed north up 13 in hot pursuit but haven't caught up with anyone yet except one rancher with a truckload of hay. Are you on the road yet?"

He listened to a long explanation of the police action and what to do if he encountered the kidnappers. He made a series of comments, along with *yes, sir* and *no, sir* answers, and then hung up the phone.

"OK, we're to continue to try to catch up to these guys and locate Julie." Jeff summarized the conversation for Rich. "The chief contacted the police in Meeker and asked them to set up a roadblock just south of town so that they can't get into town. He expects them to just drive into his roadblock, but that assumes they don't know the local roads at all."

"What about Piceance Creek Road?" asked Rich. "That leads up onto the plateau. They could hide away up there in any of a hundred little draws and gulches."

"Yeah, you're right. But the Charger can't get up the small dirt roads very well."

"Unless they have another car up there. Or a Jeep."

"Well, I hope that's not goin' to happen."

The truck was screeching along the blacktop as fast as Jeff could go, given the turns and small hills they had to climb. He had to cut his speed to about sixty as the sun began to settle behind the western mountains that formed the edge of the Roan Plateau. The valley fell into shadow, but it was still bright enough to see well. That would change soon.

As they came to the turnoff for Piceance Creek Road, they had to switch on their headlights. The west side of the valley was already getting dark, even though the crest of the hogback on the eastern side still caught the last rays of a deep-orange sunset.

"Wait, I see taillights up the creek. It might be them," Rich called out as he strained to see the portion of the road that ran up a side valley into Piceance Creek. "Hold up a minute."

"I can't just stop here. They might be ahead of us."

"But that might have been them." Rich craned his neck to look out the rear window of the truck's cab. "Stop and back up a little ways. Maybe I can still see them."

Jeff hit the brakes and skidded to a stop. "This had better be good, Rich. Or they might get away." He threw the gearshift into reverse and backed up as fast as possible in the dim light. He had to be careful not to veer into the opposing lane and catch some other driver coming around the corner unaware.

"There, I see the lights again," Rich said eagerly. "I think those are Charger taillights, Jeff."

Jeff strained his eyes to see the red lights in the distance, just going around the bend in the road. "Well, you might be right. They do look like a Charger, but at this distance, I'm not sure."

Just then, Jeff's phone beeped. "Hey, Chief." He listened for a moment. "Yeah, they should be in Meeker by now if they were hauling ass . . . But wait. We think we saw their taillights headed up County 5, Piceance Creek Road . . . Well, I can't be too sure. We just caught a glimpse as they started up the grade . . . We're stopped here at the turnoff."

Rich slapped his hand on the dashboard, agitated by the lost time and frustrated by being cut out of the conversation. "Let's get moving."

"Why don't we chase the car we just saw? There aren't any other county roads off 13 between here and Meeker anyway." He listened, frustration rising. "Well, let one of the Meeker guys drive down this way to look for them too. We'll go up the creek, and you can pull off when you get here. OK?" Ending the call, he rolled his eyes.

"All right," Jeff said to Rich as he gunned the engine to do a power turn across the highway. He roared back to the intersection and skidded onto Piceance Creek Road. He shifted gears and gained speed.

"So. We're going after them?"

"We're to follow and call in what we see. 'Do not attempt to apprehend the suspects.' That's what the chief said." Jeff grinned at his friend. He knew what they would both do if they caught up to the kidnappers. "Like hell."

"Well, hurry up. It's going to be completely dark soon," Rich said, concern in his voice. "We can't let them get away."

They raced up the creek valley as quickly as the old Ford would go, gaining elevation gradually and following the gentle curves of the valley floor. The valley was narrow compared to that of Government Creek, with its wide pastures and meadows. Here the valley narrowed frequently but opened onto meadows that could be up to a half mile long. Occasional small gravel roads turned off into minor valleys or gulches where the uncommon house or ranch resided.

As they drove along, they caught occasional peeks at a set of taillights receding up the valley tantalizingly ahead of them. They couldn't gain on the Charger no matter how much Jeff pushed the Ford at reckless speed. The Charger was a faster car, but it appeared that the driver was not familiar with the road. Jeff, on the other hand, had driven it many times.

"We're going to enter a series of sharp meanders comin' up soon," Jeff reminded his friend, who had also been on the road before. "They'll have to slow down as it gets completely dark and we climb up onto the plateau." He looked over at Rich, who had pulled a flashlight out of the glove box. "I hope Julie's all right. She must be scared to death."

They swung around a sharp turn and recognized the unmistakable taillights of the Charger just a half mile ahead of them. As soon as they saw the car, it vanished behind another rolling hill. Then it appeared again for a moment before again disappearing into the night.

"They're turning off on another road up there," Rich said loudly.

They made a turn onto a county gravel road and Jeff stopped. He took out his cell phone and tried to call the chief. No signal.

"We need to leave some sort of sign that we turned here. I have a flare we could use if we leave it in the road where it won't start a fire. I hope the cops figure it out."

He jumped out of the truck and ran to the toolbox in the back. He pulled out a red flare, broke off the cap to start it, and dropped it in the center of the road.

"That'll have to do," he said gruffly. "We'd better get after that car, or we'll lose them up here in the sage country." He climbed back into the truck and accelerated westward.

The road began to twist around more sharply as they entered a canyon. The tires screeched around the next turns, and they slowed down in order to navigate in the quickly forming darkness. The road climbed more steeply as it brought them to the top of the plateau. It was a broad tableland made up of undulating hills and ridges and shallow gulches and swales, all vegetated by wild grasses, shrubs, and sagebrush.

Jeff drove wildly to close the distance between themselves and the kidnappers. They gained a glimpse of the Charger again after a mile but lost it around another turn. He raced ahead and had a brief sighting of the red taillights just as they crested a ridge and dropped into a broad valley ahead. There were no lights ahead of them. They slowed down and then stopped while they were near the top of the ridge crest.

"Wait a minute," he said loudly. "We should be able to see them ahead of us here. I know this road, and we should be looking down a long curving decline to the valley floor. They should be in plain view even if they're a half mile away."

"Where in hell'd they go?" Rich scanned ahead through the windshield. "We should be right on top of them." He climbed out of the car and called to Jeff through the open window. "Shut the truck off and cut the lights a minute. Let me listen for them."

Jeff complied and then stepped out of the truck and onto the narrow blacktop road. The sun was buried behind the western edge of the broad, rolling landscape. It was dark, but the rising half-moon threw silvery light across the scene and let their eyes adjust to the haunting reality of the night.

A light breeze touched their faces and carried the scent of sagebrush and dry dust to their noses. It was completely still except for the occasional distant howl of a single coyote somewhere to their west. Perhaps he had become separated from his pack. Then they heard an engine rev on the ridge to the right of where the road passed.

"They turned off back there on the ridge," Rich whispered. "We must have missed it."

"Yeah, I think I know where they went." Jeff was already climbing into the cab. "It's that dirt road out to the old oil shale test site. Let's go."

Jeff started the truck and threw the gearshift into reverse. He made a three-point turn as quickly as he could, nearly getting the rear wheels down in the ditch by the side of the pavement. Then they shot back up the road to the ridge.

"Here. Take the phone. Try to call the chief and tell him where we are." He tossed the cell phone to Rich, then slowed down to look for the turnoff onto a narrow dusty track that had once been a busy side road.

"I can't get a signal up here," Rich said. "We're too far from a cell tower."

"Shoot," Jeff muttered. "We'll have to mark our turn somehow then, so they can find us."

"Do you have any more flares in the tool kit? Or a reflective triangle?" Rich tried to come up with ideas. "We can leave a flashlight if we have to."

"Wait," Jeff said quietly. "I have my camping lamp in the back somewhere. We can leave that at the side of the turnoff. The chief will see it for sure."

He pulled the truck onto the dirt track and climbed out of the cab with the motor running. He rummaged through his toolbox in the bed of the truck and extracted a compact lantern that was normally used to light his campsite when overnighting in the wild. He twisted a switch and the LED bulbs shone brightly. Setting it on the ground at the side of the road so that anyone coming up from the south would see it easily, he jumped back in the truck and motored forward on the dirt road.

"That should be hard to miss," he said.

They drove forward cautiously now because they had no idea how far along the route the kidnappers had gone. The road ran back to the one-story building that had housed the garage and offices for an oil shale start-up company some twenty years earlier when that was the rage for new energy resources. The company had built a demonstration site for the Department of Energy but had fallen on hard times soon after they proved they could extract oil from the dark shale beds that underlay the plateau. That was the mark of another boom-and-bust cycle that seemed to define the history of rural Colorado.

"The road only goes in for about a quarter mile to the buildings," Jeff whispered, "and then goes on farther to the test site itself. There are several wells, aboveground bulk oil tanks, and pipelines back there, giving them a lot of places to hide out if they need to."

He pulled the truck to a halt and switched off the engine. "We'd better walk the rest of the way or they'll hear us coming. Grab that handgun of yours and let's listen again." Jeff pulled his Winchester .30-.30 rifle from the rear gun rack.

They both stepped out of the cab and quietly closed the truck doors. It took a moment for their eyes to adjust to the darkness again. The moon had risen a little higher in the night sky and threw dark shadows in the bushes and low trees around them. There was no sound except for the rustle of leaves when the wind picked up.

They could see no taillights now. The kidnappers must have parked the Charger already and hidden somewhere on the site. There were no sounds to indicate where they had gone.

"We have to walk quietly up the road and be alert," Jeff whispered. "Let's check out the office building first. That's the logical place to hide."

They started forward slowly and cautiously, like they would on a nighttime hunt. Jeff led at first, covering about two hundred yards to where a wooden sign on the left side of the road indicated the name of the defunct company: Maroon Energy. They could make out the faint silhouette of a structure set back to their left.

"That's the office," Jeff said quietly. "Let's check it out. Be careful. Have your gun ready."

They crept forward again, crouching low along one side of the road. Jeff had his Winchester level-action rifle with him, and Rich had his trusty 9mm Smith & Weston. Jeff quietly racked a round into the chamber. It was hard to see the ground before them, but they could decipher the outline of bushes and the building clearly enough. They picked up a whiff of gasoline as they approached the structure.

Then they saw the shape of the Charger parked in the driveway next to the front door of the building. Nobody appeared to be near it, as far as they could tell. They looked at each other in the dark and nodded. They crept forward, each one targeting a different end of the vehicle in their approach. They stopped and listened again.

"I'm going to look in the car window. See if anyone's there," Rich said in a voice that was barely audible. "You watch the building for motion, OK?"

"OK."

Without any delay, Rich raised his head long enough to glance in the rear seat window to scan for bodies. He looked for only two seconds and then lowered his head. No one was inside.

They crouched next to the car. "They must have moved Julie into the building. Let's work our way around back of this place. They won't expect anyone to approach from that direction." Jeff pointed to his left. "At least, I hope not."

They shuffled off past the car and into the shadows along the north side of the building. From there they could see inside the darkened windows of the lower floor. There was an outdoor staircase that ran up to a balcony on the back of the building. They hid behind bushes along the north side for a few minutes to evaluate their options. There were no lights on in the office because the electricity had been shut off years ago.

Jeff was worried because they had no idea where the kidnappers were or where they were keeping Julie. He had hoped to catch the men off guard and rescue Julie before things got too dangerous. It appeared his high hopes were unfounded. By now the men may have been planning how to hold out against any rescue attempt—or worse, they might be thinking of taking advantage of their captive.

"I'm not sure what we can do, Rich. We may have to just wait for the cops to get here."

"Yeah, I was afraid of that." Rich winced. "There's isn't much we can do in the dark, especially with Julie hostage."

Just then, sirens wailed in the distance, a sure sign that the police were approaching the ridge. Then they heard the sound of cars skidding to a halt out on the creek road. There was a lot of shouting at the turnoff and then the sound of car engines roaring through the brush along the dirt road.

"Hey, look." Rich pointed at one of the upper-floor windows. "I saw a light up there."

They both watched the window and briefly saw a flicker of yellowish light in it. It looked like someone had lit a cigarette in the dark.

"Well, we know where they are now, but I'm not sure how that helps us," Jeff said. "I guess the first thing we need to do is let the cops know where we are so they don't shoot us."

"Yeah, good idea. How are we gonna do that?"

They looked at each other for a moment. There weren't a lot of options.

"Rich, why don't you work your way out around the building far enough away that the kidnappers don't see you. You can come up behind the police cars with your flashlight on and explain the situation."

"What about you? Aren't you coming too?"

"I think I should stay put and keep an eye on the back door in case they try to run for it." Jeff wasn't sure this was a good idea, but he didn't want the men to escape with their hostage. Maybe he could do something if there was trouble and an opportunity presented itself.

"I think that's a bad idea, Jeff," his friend said. "You could get shot by mistake if the police decide to storm the place."

"You'll have to warn them that I'm back here, and we'll hope for the best." Jeff nodded toward Rich. "Maybe you can bring one of the cops back here with you."

"I'll see what I can do." Rich turned to go. "I'll be a while if I go out wide, so don't do anything stupid before I get back." He grinned and slipped away into the shadows.

Jeff sat still and could hear Rich hurrying away but then lost track of him. He detected movement in the building, probably the kidnappers figuring out what they would do now that the police were arriving. He guessed that the police would try to contact the fugitives and negotiate. That's what they were trained to do in a hostage situation like this. It would be the smart move given that it was as dark as hell and that they needed to bring in more resources before they could charge the building. It would be a good ploy to while away the night and wait until daylight was on their side. On the other hand, the kidnappers knew that once the sun came up, they couldn't sneak away as easily as they could now. They would have to surrender or fight it out.

Jeff wondered how a simple liquor store robbery had managed to escalate to a standoff like this. It was just his luck that he would happen on the scene and that it would lead to Julie being a hostage. He felt sorry for her and her bad fortune that night.

The sound of several cars hitting their brakes out on the gravel road came to his ears. It sounded like the backup troops had arrived, with car doors slamming and men shouting back and forth as they got organized. He was worried that the cops would come in too quickly and panic the fugitives. That would be bad news because they might feel like they should take a shot at a cop if they were threatened. Once shooting began, all bets were off, and Julie would be in even more danger. Chief Walters was not the kind of guy who would hesitate to shoot back.

He heard footsteps in the building. The men inside were aware of the arrival of the police cruisers and were likely getting worried. He wondered what he would do if he were trapped in a similar situation. It would be frightening to know you were soon to be outnumbered and probably have to fight your way out. You would have to use your hostage as your only leverage, which might make things worse.

If it was him, he would probably let the hostage go and sneak off into the night. A hostage would just slow him down, so it would be better to leave her inside to be discovered by the police, who would likely be very slow to enter the building and find out you were gone already. But then again, he knew the area and knew how to move through this kind of landscape. These bad guys may not be familiar with the terrain or know how to be stealthy.

He realized that either way, the kidnappers would probably try to sneak out the back of the building before they were trapped inside. That meant they would likely come down the staircase at the back of the structure any minute now. That might give Jeff a chance to rescue Julie.

He carefully tiptoed through the shadows to the base of the staircase. It was made of two-by-eight boards with an open space between the steps. He could hide underneath and wait for the men to come down to the ground, biding his time for an opportunity.

A door creaked open above Jeff's head, then he heard a footstep on the landing.

"It looks clear," a man whispered. "Bring her out. I'll drop down first to be sure we're alone." Then he heard heavy steps on the stairs as a man cautiously descended. Then other steps on the landing and a muffled cry. Julie.

Jeff hunched down into the shadows behind the steps, waiting.

The first man, Hank, stepped onto the ground right in front of Jeff, who now wished he had a handgun and not the rifle. He began to sweat in the cool evening air, afraid to give his position away.

Hank said, "OK. We're clear. Come on down." With that, he began to walk away from the stairs toward the back of the property where the abandoned well field was located. The second man, Wiley, tried to hurry down the stairs but was impeded by his hostage, who he seemed to be holding on to tightly and using as a shield. He paused when they reached the second step from the bottom, maybe to look around for danger.

Jeff saw two pairs of feet right in front of him on the step. He raised up from his crouch, still under the stairs, and reached out for Wiley's feet just as he began to step down again. He held on tight and Wiley began to fall, taking Julie with him. Wiley shouted, "What the . . . ?"

Jeff stepped out from around the base of the stairs as Wiley landed on the gravel path that led away from the steps. Both he and Julie hit the ground hard, and Wiley let go of her as he tried to break his fall. Jeff was on him before he could get up and hit the man in the back of the head with the butt end of his rifle. Wiley let out a muffled sound and fell onto the gravel unconscious.

Hank spun around at the sound of the stumble and shouted, "What's happening?" Then he saw Jeff and shot his handgun at him, missing twice as Jeff threw himself to the side of the path.

"Stay down, Julie," Jeff called out as he rolled over once and lined up a shot. "Better run for it, mister, or I'll drop you right here!" he shouted and fired one round at Hank. The rifle roared, and the slug hit Hank's leg. That was enough to send Hank hobbling away into the dark in the direction of the well field.

Jeff crawled to Julie and turned her over to look at her. He pulled off the tape that covered her mouth. "Are you OK, Jules? Are you hurt?"

"Jeff, is that you? I can't see anything with this thing over my eyes," she said softly as she sat up. "Is it safe?"

"Yeah. Here, let me get this off you." He lifted the blindfold and began to untie her hands, then pulled her to him for a hug. "It's safe now. But we should get under cover." He helped her to her feet and led her into the bushes to hide.

Just then, they heard the police chief on a bullhorn. "This is Chief Walters speaking. We know you're in there. Stop shooting and come out with your hands up."

Two spotlights from the police cruisers suddenly lit up the front of the building. Police were apparently getting into position to surround the place. The chief continued. "Who are you, and where is the hostage? We want to negotiate with you. It isn't too late to stop this before anyone gets hurt. Now come out and release the hostage."

Jeff heard the sounds of someone approaching through the brush to his left. The person was trying to be stealthy but was not succeeding. Jeff put his finger up to Julie's mouth to indicate that she should stay silent. He gripped the rifle and pointed it in the direction of the sound.

"Jeff?" Rich called out quietly. "You here? It's me, Rich."

"Over here, Rich," Jeff said loudly, lowering the rifle. "I'm in the brush with Julie. Don't shoot."

A flashlight beam scanned the area and finally stopped moving when it illuminated their pale faces. Jeff turned on his cell phone flashlight feature to show where he was.

"I have Officer Crowley with me. We're to hold the perimeter." Rich came close and saw Julie crouched next to Jeff. "Jeez! Julie. Are you OK? How'd you get free?"

"Wait a minute," Crowley said, surprised. "I thought you were kidnapped."

"I was," Julie said mournfully. "Jeff got me free." She began to tear up.

"Hey, you guys," Jeff said. "I knocked out one of the kidnappers over there. Why don't you cuff him, and I can take Julie back to the cars."

"OK. Show me where he is," Crowley said and followed Jeff and Julie back to the staircase.

They arrived at the stairs, and Crowley saw the man lying there. "Is he shot? Did you shoot him?" He looked up in surprise. "You didn't kill him, did you?"

"Oh, hell no. I just hit him with my rifle butt in self-defense. Then I untied Julie." Jeff looked out toward the well field. "The other guy ran off that way. I *did* shoot him in the leg after he shot at me. Luckily, he missed."

"I guess so," Crowley said. "I'll call the chief to let him know what happened and to get some other men up here." He stepped aside and pulled the handheld radio from his belt. He gave the chief an update, discussing what to do next, then came back to talk to the trio.

"OK," he said. "The chief is going to have men enter the building to clear it and then they'll come back here. And you can tell the chief what you told me."

"Aren't you going after the bad guy?" Rich asked in disbelief.

"Yes, but we have to confirm what you said first," Crowley said. "Don't worry. He's not going to get very far in the dark. We need more men to hunt him down if he gets to the well field. We might have to wait until dawn anyway, just to be safe."

They stood by and waited for fifteen minutes while Jeff examined Julie's wrists and face. She had been tied up tight, and the rope had worn her skin badly, bruising and tearing it in places. Her face was turning black and blue on the right side where she had landed at the bottom of the stairs. Her throat was red, and she had a huge bump on the other side of her head.

"I'm really sorry you landed like that, Jules. I didn't want to hurt you in any way," Jeff said. "I just had a chance to stop that guy, and so I did it without thinking how it would hurt you. I'm sorry for that."

"Don't apologize for rescuing me, cowboy. I'm glad to be free of those goons. They didn't hurt me much, but I was afraid they might rape me or something if they had me overnight." She teared up again. "I was real scared, Jeff." She put her head on his shoulder and cried openly. He enclosed her in his arms and held her.

"It'll be OK, Jules. Don't worry." He felt very close to her then and knew she would be safe.

Chief Walters appeared out of the dark with a flashlight and shook Jeff's hand. "Good work, Jeff. Are you OK? Crowley said you exchanged fire with one of these outlaws. No hits?"

"No, I'm fine." Jeff reached up and touched his ear, which was beginning to sting suddenly. His hand came away with blood on it. "What the hell?"

Julie held the cell phone up to illuminate his face and looked at his ear. Then she gasped.

"I think that man shot you in the ear, Jeff. There's a notch out of it here." She poked it and he cringed.

"Yow, that hurt."

"OK, you three go back to the cruiser with Crowley and wait there," the chief said. "I have an ambulance on the way. Let them take a look at both of you." He turned toward Rich. "How about you? Any wounds to report?"

"No, sir."

"Then get going. We've got it from here."

By that time six lawmen had gathered around them, reporting that they had found no one else in the building. The chief split his men into three teams of two each, and they spread out in the direction of the well field. Then the trio and Crowley walked to the front of the structure, where all the police vehicles had parked haphazardly along the dirt road.

An ambulance arrived a half hour later and was unable to make its way up the narrow dirt road. They walked out to meet the emergency technicians at their vehicle. The techs patched up Julie's wrists and swabbed her face with disinfectant. They stuck a gauze bandage on Jeff's ear, making jokes about how he would have a notch out of his ear like they used to mark cattle on the range.

Crowley released them, and they piled into Jeff's truck for the long drive home.

***

A week later Rich showed up at Jeff's house with a twelve-pack of Colorado Native in one hand and a DVD in his other hand. "*Fast & Furious 6*, guys!" he called out. "And I smell pizza already."

Julie met him at the door and gave him a hug. "Welcome to our place, Rich. We're going to have some fun tonight."

He walked into the kitchen where Jeff had pulled the pizza out of the oven to test it. He turned around and shook hands with his buddy. He pushed the pizza back into the oven and set a timer. "Just a few more minutes. Let's crack a beer and celebrate."

Jeff reached up to scratch his ear but hesitated when he touched the gauze that still covered the notch. He smiled at his friends and especially at his new roommate and lover, Julie. They all made a toast.

"To fast times and free living!" Jeff said.

"And good men and fine beer," Julie said, as they clinked their bottles together.

"I'll drink to that," Rich said. "And to exciting lives for us all."

Chasing Cattle

Luke raised himself up in the saddle to get a better view of the terrain ahead. He patted his horse, Jerry, on the neck as he surveyed the landscape. He was looking at low rolling hills with occasional low peaks scattered about, some with rocky crags projecting from their sides or forming stand-alone outcrops. Some were big enough to create their own little hills where the bedrock protruded up from the dry grass meadows surrounding them.

It was a hazy afternoon in southeastern Wyoming that day, sunny but also smoky due to wildfires burning in the mountains farther west. The smoke carried a thousand miles to reach this part of the country, and it gave an edge to the already dry summer air. Worse, it made looking for Annabelle even more difficult. He knew she was out there somewhere, and he and his ranch hand buddy José had to find her before nightfall.

Annabelle, number 347, was one of the older cows in the herd of beef that belonged to the Bar-R-Star-M Ranch that Luke worked for. She was last seen a few days before when the herd had been feeding in Spring Creek Valley just two miles away. Now the herd had moved east, and she apparently had not. One of the ranch hands had noticed her absence the day before when he came out to feed the herd grain near the creek. The hand had counted only 241 cattle instead of the expected 242. The foreman had come to double check the count and noticed that Annabelle was missing.

"How the heck did Blake know that animal three forty-seven was missing?" Luke asked as he scanned the horizon. "I mean, out of so many cows?"

"You're still learning about this business, amigo." José chuckled. "She was expected to drop her calf any day, and they were keeping a special eye on her. She's one of those secret birthing types. She's been known to hide her calf from the herd."

"You're kidding me," Luke said. "Why would she do that? Not stick with the herd?"

"Some cows must think having a calf is private. I don't know. Anyway, some cows do that for a few days to protect their young one."

"And now we have to find out where she's playing hide-and-seek. Great." Luke turned in his saddle to face José and grinned. "Have you been at the ranch so long as to know which cow is which?"

José gave Luke a cockeyed look. "Hey, I been cattle doggin' for a while, both here at the Bar-R-Star-M and farther north. I know about this ranch and its history. I've been doing it for years. How come you're asking dumb questions?"

"I've been out on the range mostly, away from ranches. You know, not part of the daily activities like raising calves and that sort of stuff."

"You're just green, that's all." José tightened his reins and looked west at a low rocky ridge that rose higher than most of the others. "Let's get up there and see what we can see. I have an idea where she may have gone to be by herself."

"OK. At least we'll have a good view all around," Luke said as he pulled the reins left to situate Jerry to face west and follow José. His horse responded and stepped forward after he turned. Luke spurred the horse lightly with his heels, and the bay broke into a canter. Jerry's ears pricked up as he sighted ahead toward the ridge. They settled into a steady three-beat gait and covered the distance easily. The ground was soft due to the recent rains, and there were no prairie dog holes to worry about. In ten minutes they were on the ridge and had a complete view of half the ranch's twenty-eight thousand acres.

José pulled his horse up on the highest point and began to dig in his right saddlebag for an old pair of army surplus binoculars. He let his horse's reins have some slack as he began to scan the valley just below them to the north. "One year when old Annabelle had a calf, she held up in this valley for three days. She had lots of grass, water in the creek, and some privacy." He continued to search for the cow while speaking. "But she never seems to go to the same place twice, just similar places with water and grass."

"So how do we find her? Check all the valleys?"

"No. We have to think like a cow." José grinned. "She wouldn't walk too far because she was pregnant and fat. So she's maybe here or in that next valley over there." He pointed farther north. "We can check this one out and then ride to the next one if we need to. But we don't have a lot of time before dark."

"OK. Let's go," Luke said as he lifted his reins to follow José.

The started out walking down the slope on a diagonal, taking it easy on their mounts' legs on the descent. As they rode along, Luke sidled closer to José's horse to talk.

"Say, how well do you know Blake?" Luke asked cautiously. "You've been here awhile. Is he pretty easygoing?"

"Are we talking about our boss, the foreman?" José glanced sideways at Luke. "You know him. He's as tough as nails and very demanding." He looked at his young friend. "Didn't Blake chew you out for being late last week? You ought to know he doesn't take to slackers."

Luke felt like the *slacker* term had been misapplied to his lateness that day. He cringed and was silent for a minute as they reached the valley floor. José regarded him suspiciously for a while and then said, "Wait a minute. Why are you asking about Blake anyway? It doesn't have to do with his daughter Samantha, does it?"

Luke looked surprised by that question. He didn't think he was being so obvious. "No, no. Not Samantha. No way. She's kinda old anyway."

"Old? She's only twenty-eight or so. She's one good-looking woman to my thinking. She did have that failed marriage but that wasn't her fault." José pulled his horse up to stop. He stared at Luke with a straight face.

Luke stopped right next to him and looked sheepish. He started to sweat, even though it wasn't that hot in the valley, and avoided eye contact with José.

"Oh my God," José said loudly. "You're thinking about Katie? Blake's younger daughter?" An incredulous look spread across his face. "You must be crazy, cowboy. She's his baby girl. She's only seventeen or eighteen, if I remember right. He's very protective of her."

"Yeah, I figured. She seems special to him, being so young and all." Luke stared at his saddle horn. "She's real nice, though. We talked at the barn dance last week, and she seemed pretty neat to me."

José shook his head and looked angry. "You better think real hard about this, cowboy. It's serious business when you work for the girl's father. You could make the man mad as hell if he catches you and her together."

"No. It ain't like that," Luke said hurriedly. "I mean, we only talked once."

José shook his head again and looked out at the side of the valley behind them. He reacted like something had surprised him.

"Hey. Look up there." He pointed across the valley at a rock outcrop. "There's a cow up there, and she might be Annabelle." He turned to head up the slope toward the rocks. "Let's check it out."

They both fell into a canter again and crossed the quarter mile in about two minutes, catching up with the cow near the rock outcrop. The cow appeared frantic and was walking back and forth next to a crevasse in the rocky slope of the mountain. She mooed loudly and seemed hoarse from the effort. She had an ear tag that read 347. A faint cry came from the crevasse.

"Yep. It's Annabelle, all right," José said with certainty as he dismounted and walked over to look in the crevasse, a long, narrow slot in the rock where the outcrop had pulled away from the rest of the hillside. It varied from about one foot to two feet wide and thirty feet long, with an uneven bottom that graded toward them. Ten feet deep at the nearest end, it dropped to more than twenty feet deep farther away. Near the bottom of the crevasse, a frightened brown calf stood on unstable legs. It looked at José in surprise and called again for its mama.

"Hey, Luke," he said. "We've got a calf over here." He turned to motion his companion over.

"Wow! How'd he get in there?" Luke asked as he eyed the forlorn creature. "It's pretty narrow in there. Not more than a foot wide in spots."

"I don't know, but what I do know is that I can't fit in there." José scanned up and down Luke's thin frame. "But I think you can get in there if we lower you down on a rope."

"What? No way I'd be able to even move around in there." Luke looked all along the rocky slot. "Well, maybe if I can get down over there, I can sidle over to the little fella." He walked out along the outcrop to look at how its width changed. "Yeah. Maybe here." He scrambled ahead. "And I can move over there, I think." He looked back at his buddy and shrugged.

By that time Annabelle had pushed up close to peer into the crack again and nudged José over to get a better look. The cow mooed loudly in desperation. She turned to José and seemed to ask for his help in an indirect manner. Maybe she had been around humans enough to know they weren't the enemy most of the time. Sometimes they did nice things like bring food and aid.

"Don't worry, Annabelle," José muttered to her in low tones. "We'll get your baby out of there."

The two men sprang into action, each getting his lariat off his saddle and setting up a towline. They had to tie the two ropes together to be long enough to reach out to the crevasse and still reach back to a place where José's horse, Jasper, could move forward. At the same time, Luke tied an extra short length of rope around his waist with a loop knotted off around each leg. When he finished, he had two leg loops and a waist loop tied off so that they wouldn't tighten when he put weight on the harness. Then he ran the end of the lariat through all the loops of the seat harness and tied it off in a bowline knot. Pulling up on the lariat, he checked to see if the harness would keep him hanging straight when lowered into the narrow space of the crevasse.

"You about set?" José called from next to Jasper, who now had the end of the combined ropes tied to his saddle horn. He led Jasper forward until the slack was out of the rope. "I'll have Jasper back up slowly when you're ready."

After a quick test of the rope, Luke tossed his Stockade hat on the ground and stepped over to a wide spot in the crevasse just over the calf. Then he leaned back and lowered himself over the edge of the rock. His hips just made it into the crevasse when the rope pulled tight and held him in place.

"OK. Lower away. I'll slide down the side. Be ready to stop if I call out. I may get twisted up if I hit a narrow ledge in here."

José backed Jasper up carefully so as not to drop his sidekick too quickly. He had used his horse and rope to create a makeshift elevator like this before, but not to lower someone into a crack in the earth. Luke called out when he needed to slow down.

Luke found the crevasse a tight fit because he had to get his hips and shoulders past bulges in the rock walls while moving lower. He looked down and saw the calf almost below him, gazing up like some weird creature from another world was coming at him. He hadn't seen humans before this and probably didn't much like the looks of one dropping in on top of him.

"It's OK, little fella. We're goin' to get you out of here and back with your mama." Luke tried to keep the animal calm but wasn't sure the little guy would tolerate sharing the crack with him.

Annabelle stood at the end of the crevasse, where she could see at least part of her offspring, and mooed nervously. That caused the calf to wander along the crack toward her call. Luke tried to shift his trajectory in the same direction, but Jasper lowered him to the bottom of the crevasse. At that point the calf was twelve feet from where Luke landed on his feet.

"Hold it there a minute, José," Luke called out. "I've got to move to my right and shift the rope over on the rim."

José appeared at the top of the crack and checked on Luke. He helped move the rope toward the calf's new position. Luke sidestepped his way toward the calf as it called out mournfully for its mom. Reaching the calf, he had enough room to grab him and get his arms under his front legs. When he picked up the calf, it led to maaing and grunting on the animal's part. Luke had a hard time holding on to him as the calf squirmed to get free.

"OK. I got him, José. Take up the slack and get us out of here."

José returned to Jasper and slowly led him forward. Luke began to lift off the bottom of the crack and swung sideways in the narrow space. The weight of the calf wriggling in his arms caused him to pitch forward so that the animal was just below him and his torso was horizontal. He couldn't look up to see where they were going as the rope dragged them bodily against the rock wall. At one point it was so tight that Luke thought they would get stuck right there. But Jasper kept on tugging away, and they squeezed past the narrow spot.

He almost dropped the calf then and lost his purchase under one leg. He had to struggle to keep his grip. Meanwhile, the rope harness was cutting into his legs. He was at the top of the crevasse and had no place to go. The rope just tightened up as the horse tried to drag him sideways.

"Stop! Stop!" he shouted. "I'm up top. Come help me with this critter, will ya?"

José came over and looked at Luke's back. "What you doin' upside down there, cowboy? I was looking for your head to come up first."

"Jeez, José. Just pull me up a bit and take this little guy from me, will ya?" Luke grunted. "I'm about to lose my grip on him."

José knelt down and reached under Luke's shoulders to grab an arm and pull up. Once Luke got a shoulder over the edge, he could right himself enough to pass the calf up to his buddy. With his hands up on either side of the crevasse, he threw his body up onto terra firma. He lay on his back and tried to catch his breath while José carried the crying calf over to Annabelle, who was mooing frantically and trotting back and forth by the edge of the outcrop.

After a few minutes, Luke stood up and took off the harness. He and José watched the hungry calf as he partook of a long overdue snack of fresh milk. Annabelle licked her baby and nuzzled it the whole time.

"The sun's getting low. I guess we better get this show on the road," José said jovially. "How about you sling the calf over the saddle across your lap, and we'll let Annabelle follow behind. I don't think the calf can walk all the way back to the ranch on his little legs yet."

"OK. Sure." Luke coiled up his lariat and tucked the extra piece of rope in his saddlebag. He mounted up, and José handed up the calf for him to hold. Luke arranged the calf as José climbed up on Jasper. They set off at a walk so that Annabelle could keep up. The cow seemed to know where they were headed and trotted alongside, mooing to her offspring as she went. The calf looked at her but didn't struggle to get down, probably too tired to resist his fate.

"We should name this little fella," Luke said happily. "We could call him Explorer or something like that."

"Explorer? I like it." José laughed. "But I think we'd better let Katie decide on that. It's her calf, after all."

"What? Are you kidding me?" Luke asked in surprise. "How's it her calf?"

"Well, Annabelle is Katie's cow from her 4-H project. She plans to show this little guy, along with his mother, this summer at the fair. It's her last year to enter."

"Why didn't you tell me this before? I mean that it was Katie's cow we were looking for?"

"I don't know. I didn't think it was important." José chuckled. "But Katie will be excited to see this little guy. She'll probably be real happy with us for bringing her calf back. She was very worried about it this morning before we set out."

"Maybe I can take the calf right to her." Luke grinned at José. "Then I can ask her to the dance on Saturday."

José just grinned. "Don't get ahead of yourself there, cowboy."

They rode slowly across the last ridge and looked down on the ranch house and barn. The sun was just dipping beneath the hills to the west. It had turned out to be a pretty good day for all involved. Suddenly Luke's romantic prospects were looking up. He grinned and patted the calf on its neck as he thought about what to say to Katie.

About the Author

Fred G. Baker is a hydrologist, historian, and writer living in Colorado. He is the author of *The Final Wave, Lena's Secret War, Einstein's Raven, ZONA: The Forbidden Land, The Black Freighter,* the *Modern Pirate* series of short and long stories, and the *Detective Sanchez/Father Montero Mysteries* series. He is also the author of nonfiction works such as *Growing Up Wisconsin, The Life and Times of Con James Baker,* and *The Light from a Thousand Campfires* (with Hannah Pavlik).

***

Request for Reviews

Thank you for reading my book. If you enjoyed it, I invite you to write a review on Amazon.com. Reviews are important to help authors get the word out about their work, and I would appreciate your taking the time to write one.

Please look for my other books on Amazon and Kindle Books. Just type in Fred G. Baker to see other titles that may be of interest to you. You can also check out my website at www.othervoicespress.com.

Made in the USA
Thornton, CO
06/11/22 16:45:39